Misfortune's Favourite

Srinivas Rao Adige, educated at The Doon School, Dehradun and St Stephen's College, New Delhi, has worked for the Indian Administrative Service. A keen student of Indian history, he combines his passion for the past with his flair for writing. Adige is married and lives in New Delhi.

Also by the author
The Mughal High Noon: The Ascent of Aurangzeb

Misfortune's Favourite

THE TRAGIC END OF
DARA SHUKOH

SRINIVAS RAO ADIGE

RUPA

Published by
Rupa Publications India Pvt. Ltd 2022
7/16, Ansari Road, Daryaganj
New Delhi 110002

Sales centres:
Allahabad Bengaluru Chennai
Hyderabad Jaipur Kathmandu
Kolkata Mumbai

This is a work of fiction. All situations, incidents, dialogue and characters,
with the exception of some well-known historical and public figures mentioned
in this novel, are products of the author's imagination and are not to be
construed as real. They are not intended to depict actual events or people or
to change the entirely fictional nature of the work. In all other respects, any
resemblance to persons living or dead is entirely coincidental.

ISBN: 978-93-5520-546-9

First impression 2022

10 9 8 7 6 5 4 3 2 1

The moral right of the author has been asserted.

Printed in India

To André and Urshila

One

With weary steps, and in the last stages of physical exhaustion, Dara Shukoh dragged himself up the ornate staircase late that night and crossed the open courtyard leading to the private apartments of his palace in Agra Fort. As a gaggle of terrified palace eunuchs parted the heavy draperies at its entrance, Dara staggered in. The ladies-in-waiting who were fanning his consort Nadira Banu Begum and their daughter Jahanzeb Bano recoiled in horror at seeing their prince, Emperor Shah Jahan's eldest son and putative heir to the Mughal throne, otherwise so immaculately and regally dressed, with his flashing eye and benign smile, now in such a dishevelled and woebegone condition, which the myriads of lighted lamps in the chamber did little to conceal. Nadira stepped forward swiftly, her brows furrowed with concern, and steadied her husband, scarcely noticing his broad forehead, the long straight nose, the drooping moustache and the beard that hid a pursed mouth. His receding chin betrayed more than a hint of irresolution and indecisiveness. She gently eased him onto a divan as he laid aside his jewel-encrusted sword and removed his helmet while his trusted eunuch Khwaja Maqbool undid the heavy steel breast plate that covered his torso.

'All is lost,' Dara mumbled brokenly, his chin resting on his chest, not daring to look his wife in the eye, as he sat slumped on the divan with drooping shoulders. Then eventually raising his head, which was dripping with perspiration in the wilting heat of the North Indian plains in high summer, and looking at Nadira with defeat writ large in his eyes, he rasped through parched lips, 'Our forces…have been routed…Siphir and I along with a few followers…managed to flee…' Dara practically choked as he said these words. 'Aurangzeb's and Murad's men…are at the gates of Agra…'

'Quick…some water…' Nadira turned and signalled to one of her ladies-in-waiting.

As the girl fled to carry out the bidding, Nadira drew out a handkerchief from her sleeve and gently mopped her husband's brow and face.

Much before Dara and their younger son Siphir had reached the gates of the fort after fleeing from the battlefield of Samugarh, barely eight kos from Agra, where Emperor Shah Jahan was temporarily residing, word had reached the palace that the imperial forces, led by Dara, had been decisively defeated. With Shah Jahan persuaded by Dara not to take the field in person, and Shah Shuja, the second of the Emperor's four sons, still smarting from his defeat at the hands of Dara's eldest son, Sulaiman, near Benares, in a vain attempt to seize the throne, and then retreating hastily eastwards towards his viceroyalty in Bengal, and Sulaiman himself too far away from Samugarh to be able to assist his father, power had effectively passed in the Mughal heartland into the hands of Shah Jahan's other two sons, Aurangzeb and Murad Bakhsh, who had rebelled against their father.

As the girl returned with a goblet of iced water, and Nadira gently held it to Dara's lips, panic seized her, but she steeled herself. This was not the time to display even the slightest trace of weakness. 'How is Siphir? I hope to Allah that no harm has come to him,' she asked, trying to keep her voice as steady as possible.

Dara drank the water in great gulps and held out the goblet for more. Nadira took it from his hand and then gave it to the girl for a refill. Before Dara could answer, Siphir, all of fourteen, with the first few hair beginning to sprout on his face, lurched in, looking equally exhausted. He moved towards Nadira, who enveloped him in her arms.

'Allah be praised, you are safe,' she said. 'Let me look at you. What is this? You are wounded,' she cried as she saw the gash on his arm.

'It is nothing, Mother,' he replied, trying to sound brave. 'Only a superficial scratch. It will heal in no time. You know, I parried the thrust of a Deccani cavalryman and sent him to hell.'

'Let me apply some medicine to your wound,' said Nadira as she signalled to a lady-in-waiting to fetch a basin full of water, some bandages and a jar of ointment.

Siphir went and sat by his father's side.

'Well done, Brother,' Jahanzeb, five years younger than Siphir, exclaimed. 'You have fought and shed blood for a just cause.'

'What about Sulaiman?' asked Nadira, turning to Dara. 'He has defeated Shuja in battle and surely he can come to our aid.'

'Yes, but that was near Benares. At present, he is at least two weeks' march away from here, even by the quickest means possible. If he is to bring his cannon up to give battle, it will take him even longer, while Aurangzeb and Murad are at our doorstep,' murmured Dara weakly. 'Later perhaps he may be able to aid us, but right now, he is too far away.'

Just then one of the palace eunuchs came into the chamber. 'Your Highness, a courier from Nawab Dawood Khan waits outside. He has an urgent message for Your Royal Highness.'

Dara picked himself up tiredly and went outside. He forced himself to walk to the far end of the courtyard and then down the staircase where the courier sent by Dawood Khan, commander of the household troops, escorted by two palace attendants, was waiting. As the shadows had lengthened over the battlefield earlier that evening and the outcome of the battle was becoming increasingly apparent, and several crack regiments of the imperial army were either dissolving or deserting in droves to the enemy, it was Dawood Khan's men under whose leadership a series of protective rings had been thrown around Dara, as they resisted the enemy to the death and had escorted him and his son out of the battlefield.

The courier who had come straight from the battlefield reached into his sweat-stained tunic and with a trembling hand, pulled out a piece of paper. The message was terse. 'Very little time left...presently, enemy engaged in looting and too exhausted to pursue, but respite only temporary...suggest royal party proceed to Delhi immediately escorted by loyal cavalry squadrons under Karim Khan detailed at fort's northern gate with carriages and horses. Numbers be kept to minimum. Inshallah I shall join en route.'

To Dara, the writing on the wall was clear. There was now no other alternative except to take flight to avoid capture by his two brothers Aurangzeb and Murad. He knew what fate would befall him if he fell into their hands. Perhaps he could expect some generosity from Murad, but from Aurangzeb he was sure that there would be none. Incarceration; confiscation of all his wealth and properties; despoliation of his womenfolk and children; daily, petty humiliation; slow poisoning through the forcible administration of posta; possible blinding; and the trial and conviction by a rigged court of qazis after being declared an apostate for his consorting with unbelievers and for his efforts to find a common ground between Islam and Hinduism, followed by sentencing and execution—he could visualize it all in his mind's eye. No fate could be worse than that. Moreover, despite the defeat, was there still not a good chance of him being able to rouse the garrisons in Delhi and Lahore to his cause, and reclaim the empire in the name of his father by mounting a counterattack and taking back Agra, while Sulaiman engaged the rebel forces by advancing from the east? For the present, however, escape from the fort was imperative, before the enemy got any closer and it was necessary to alert the others who would be accompanying him to prepare for the flight. Dismissing the messenger with instructions to inform Dawood Khan that the party consisting of around a dozen persons would be ready in two watches, i.e. approximately four hours, he was just turning back to return to his private apartments when another attendant arrived and conveyed that the court chamberlain urgently sought an audience.

Dara waited as the court chamberlain came up to him. 'His Majesty desires My Lord's presence urgently,' said the court chamberlain as he bowed and then withdrew.

Dara nodded. He was faced with a grave dilemma. He would be failing in his duty as a son if he did not appear before his father when summoned. Yet, burdened with the shame and humiliation of having been defeated by his younger brothers, he could not find the courage to face the Emperor. After all, he had gone into battle leading the flower of the Mughal army against those whom he had himself described as a ragtag bunch of Deccani rebels, and had promised Shah Jahan an easy victory. What was he to say to his father now? What excuse could he offer? Would it not be better if he just slunk away, unnoticed and unsung, till in God's good time he was able to retrieve his fortunes and deliver the rebels a blow from which they could never recover?

'What tidings does the messenger bring?' asked Nadira anxiously as she saw Dara entering the apartment with a downcast look, just as she was finishing bandaging Siphir's wound.

'We have very little time before Aurangzeb and Murad reach the gates of the fort,' replied Dara tiredly, avoiding any mention of the Emperor's summons. There is not a moment to lose. We shall have to move to Delhi and carry on the fight from there. Pray to Allah that its governor, Zulfiqar Baksh, does not betray us. Nawab Dawood Khan is detailing a strong escort party to accompany us on the journey. He will join us later. Luckily, the surrounding countryside is loyal, but how long they will remain so, once news of our defeat spreads, one cannot say.' Pointing to the water clock that stood in a corner of the chamber, he sighed. 'We shall leave within two watches from now. Only the bare essentials must be carried and the numbers in the party will have to be kept to the absolute minimum.'

'Two watches? Have you any idea how long it will take to pack? How can we get ready for the journey in so short a time?' Nadira expostulated. 'Even reaching Delhi by the quickest means possible will take at least seven days. And suppose Zulfiqar Baksh does not open his gates for us. It means that we might then have to travel even further. No, two watches to prepare for such a long journey is quite impossible. We will need more time. Moreover, should we not take leave of our elders properly? Surely you would like to pay your respects to the Emperor before we take our leave. Noor-e-Zamani Roshanara Begum is still on her way back from Kashmir, but I am sure Mallika-e-Zamani Jahanara Begum, who has stood by us all this while, and who is here, would like to see you before we leave. She would take it amiss if we did not do so.'

At Roshanara's name being taken, Dara's mouth tightened. There was no love lost between the two, for he was aware that his sister was identified with the clique that was opposed to him in the Mughal court. Besides, her attempts to turn Shah Jahan's mind against him for his night-long discussions with Hindu religious savants, even going so far as to have their holy book, the Bhagavad Gita, translated into Farsi, had not been lost on him, or indeed on others in the court, by the Emperor's seemingly casual remarks on more than one occasion.

'There is no time for all that,' replied Dara harshly, a mixture of rage and despair evident in his voice as he looked at Nadira. 'Don't you realize that the enemy is practically at the gates and we have very little time if we are to leave the fort precincts safely to continue the battle? Otherwise, we will all be trapped inside and you can imagine what our fate will be if that happens. Carry only that which is absolutely essential and that goes for all the others who will be accompanying us. Remember, two watches and no later.' Then, taking in the look of hurt that crossed Nadira's gentle face, with the arched eyebrows and hair that framed her smooth forehead, now touched with the slightest tinge of grey, and noting the consternation amongst the ladies-in-waiting at his outburst, he softened a little, adding, 'Don't worry. We will come out of all this. Sulaiman's victorious army will be our deliverance. I shall instruct him to march on to Agra and engage his two uncles in battle while we attack with the troops from Delhi as soon as we reach there. I am sure we will be victorious and we will return to Agra in triumph. Meanwhile, I shall send His Majesty a message explaining the circumstances of our rather sudden departure. I'm sure he will understand and explain the same to the others as well.'

Aware of her husband's sudden flashes of anger and realizing the extreme strain he was in, Nadira wisely decided against saying anything which might provoke Dara further. She watched him collect his sword and walk unsteadily into the adjoining chamber, accompanied by the eunuchs carrying his other accoutrements.

All this while, Dara had been wrestling with himself as to how to respond to the Emperor's summons, of which he had made no mention to Nadira. At length, the ignominy of having to present himself before the Emperor in his present beaten state overbore everything else. No, he did not dare face his father. Sending for some parchment, a quill and a pot of ink, he scrawled a message with a trembling hand. 'With what face can this pitiable creature present himself before Your Majesty in all his shame? I beg of you not to burden yourself with thoughts of him any longer, and instead pronounce the Fatiha on this half-dead corpse as he embarks on the long journey that lies ahead of him.'

'Make sure you have it delivered to the Emperor in person,' he bade a palace attendant as he sealed the parchment and handed it to the man.

When Shah Jahan received this message, he understood the predicament of his favourite son. Summoning his trusted eunuch, Fahim, he said, 'Go and tell Shahzadeh sahib not to lose heart. Our love for him is boundless and let him be assured that in the end, he will succeed. Our grandson Sulaiman will return soon with his invincible army under that redoubtable warrior Mirza Raja Jai Singh and he is sure to put these two ingrate sons of ours to flight, who have dared to raise their sword against the throne. Shahzadeh sahib should hasten to Delhi, seize it and carry on the fight from there. Many Rajput and Jat princes will surely rally to the imperial standards if he does so. We are ordering the governor of Delhi to extend all facilities to the Shahzadeh as if we ourselves were in residence there. We are also instructing the treasury here to open its vaults to enable the Shahzadeh to help himself to whatever precious stones, gold and jewellery he requires to carry on the fight.'

On hearing what the Emperor had said, Dara supressed a short, bitter laugh. 'Seize Delhi!' Easy enough for the Emperor to say, but even suppose he did reach Delhi, would the troops and the military wherewithal at his disposal be sufficient for him to seize and hold it? Moreover, would any of the princes in these tracts now raise even a finger to uphold the Emperor's cause, when the rebels with overwhelming force were knocking at his gates? In any case, Sulaiman was now their only hope.

Sending for his aide Aftab, Dara scrawled a letter to Sulaiman.

My son,

The imperial army has been defeated at Samugarh, near Agra. When we meet, I shall tell you the reasons that led to the defeat, but your mother, brother, sister and I are now proceeding to Delhi with a strong escort party to raise an army and carry on the fight from there. Do not fear for our safety, but be ready to march on to Agra as soon as we reach Delhi and give the signal. Thereby, the rebels will be attacked from both east and west and will assuredly be defeated. You have won a great victory against one of your uncles who sought to usurp the throne. Now, you, too, should show your mettle against the other two. Remember, the fate of the empire hangs in the balance.

'Make sure that this message gets to Sahebzada Sulaiman. See that the best man is chosen to deliver it, as there are bound to be enemy patrols on the way. A hundred gold mohurs to him who delivers it,' Dara instructed.

Aftab nodded his assent, bowed and withdrew.

Meanwhile, preparations in Dara's palace for the departure were swiftly put in motion—two watches to prepare for a flight whose duration was uncertain and which might stretch indefinitely. While Dara and Siphir readied themselves for the escape, Nadira, the ladies-in-waiting and the slave girls frantically rushed hither and thither, from chamber to chamber, rummaging through the trunks holding up a garment or an article only to discard it and pick up another, undecided as to what to take and what to leave behind. At length, some order was restored. Salwar-kameezes, ghararas, blouses, jooties, undergarments, burkas, jewels, gold mohurs, cooking utensils and water bottles, all were hastily thrown into leather travelling cases and strapped with thick ox hide belts. Easy-to-carry food stuffs and condiments were packed in containers and baskets for the journey. Trusted aides were rushed to the treasury to pick up bagful of precious stones, jewels and gold mohurs. It was decided that the party would comprise eleven persons—Dara, Nadira, Siphir, Jahanzeb and three slave girls accompanied by Dara's faithful eunuch Khwaja Maqbool, his aide Aftab and two attendants. They would be escorted by other attendants carrying the luggage and flaming torches to a rear staircase which led down to a secret tunnel at the foot of the tower adjacent to Dara's palace. Halfway down the tunnel was a false wall whose stone blocks when removed, opened into a passageway not far from the northern gate of the fort.

Buckling on their breast plates and girding their swords, and having instructed their attendants as to what essentials they would carry, Dara and Siphir along with the ladies, who were covered from head-to-toe in burkas, were shepherded to the staircase leading to the mouth of the tunnel.

Suddenly, as they reached the bottom of the staircase, Nadira cried out, 'Oh, I have forgotten something.'

'Whatever it is, there is no time to go and fetch it,' said Dara with an edge in his voice. 'We are already late and we don't know how close the enemy is.'

Nadira scarcely heard her husband. 'Come with me Jahanzeb and Saira,' she told her daughter and one of the slave girls. With flying feet, they bounded up the staircase and crossed a series of courtyards to get to the chamber where Nadira kept her most precious belongings. There, in a trunk nestled beneath a heap of silks and satins was what she had come to fetch—a beautiful leather-covered album of Persian miniatures embossed and edged with gold lettering and containing an inscription in Dara's beautiful handwriting in the Nastaliq script, which stated that it was being presented by him to his nearest and dearest companion, Nadira Begum.

Clutching the album close to her chest, Nadira, accompanied by her daughter and the slave girl, ran down the way they had come to rejoin the party as Dara waited impatiently for them. Rats scurried along the floor of the tunnel, which was of beaten earth, and the light from the torches threw strange and eerie shadows on its walls, while bats, disturbed in their habitat, screeched overhead. The party had to bow low in several places to traverse the length of the tunnel till they reached the false wall. A series of hefty blows by pickaxes carried by the attendants all around the edges of the stones embedded in the wall was sufficient to dislodge some of them from their moorings and provide enough space for the members of the party to squeeze through. One by one, they came through the tunnel, into the passageway, all covered in a layer of dust. The attendants broke open the rusty lock that fastened the small wicket door in the northern gate and the party walked through it, out into the open, under a starlit sky.

'Be careful, we can't afford to suffer another injury at this time,' said Dara as one of the girls stumbled and fell on her face, her foot getting tripped by a protruding rock near the gate.

Canvas panels were raised around the gate to protect the ladies of the court from any prying eyes. The carriages had been drawn up, each with a camel in its shaft for the ladies and horses for Dara, Siphir and the male attendants. Karim Khan, the towering captain of the guard who had been assigned with the task of leading the escorting troops by Dawood Khan, bowed respectfully as Dara emerged on the other side of the gate. Then, after Dara and Siphir had mounted their horses, he stood aside as the slave girls helped the ladies to be seated in their carriages. As Saira tried to step on the footrest, she slipped. Since the other slave girls were engaged in attending to Nadira and the others, Karim Khan, who was standing close by, caught her by her slim waist. She fell against his hard, muscled chest and at that moment, her burka parted. By the light of the flaming torches that were held by the attendants, he got a glimpse of her: wide eyes, thick eyebrows, a pert nose and a short upper lip, all set in a fair, oval, pixie-like face. Saira swiftly pulled her burka to cover her face as she got into the carriage. She had seen Karim Khan in an equestrian competition of the household troops outside the fort a few months earlier and peering through the curtains of the palanquins in which the ladies of the court sat to watch such competitions, she had been smitten by his dashing good looks.

Once all the ladies were properly seated in the carriages and their curtains drawn, Karim Khan gave a signal to the accompanying cavalry squadrons, and vaulting nimbly into the saddle, led the party forward.

Their route of escape lay north-west, along the winding course of the Jamuna River, till they reached Delhi, over a hundred kos away. Barely a few kos from where they had started, they spied a party of five scouts on horseback from one of Aurangzeb's cavalry detachments on reconnaissance, who had advanced far ahead of their main units and after a wide circuitous route, were approaching them from the north.

Karim Khan, who was riding a little ahead of the others, was the first to spot them. 'We have to cut them off before they turn back and sound the alarm,' he shouted to the accompanying sowars, turning in his saddle. He drew his sword and spurred his horse forward, followed by a section of the guards. On seeing the horsemen galloping towards them, the scouts, who were armed with swords and lances, realized that they were heavily outnumbered and turned around to flee. But Karim Khan's men were too quick for them. With flashing swords, they rode into the scouts and hurled themselves upon them, swiftly surrounding them from all sides. Finding their retreat cut off, the scouts formed a circle to repel the advance and to lessen the odds by incapacitating at least some of the attackers. However, the sheer momentum of the attack, coupled with Karim Khan's strength, broke the circle. Karim Khan picked out the scout leader and spurred his horse directly at him. As he came within a sword's length of his opponent, he parried his foe's downward blow and then drawing his arm back, dealt a blow sideways which caught the man's neck just above the carotid artery and severed it. The scout's head fell limply against his chest and then with a gurgle, he toppled from the saddle, one foot still dangling in the stirrup, as blood spurted from the fatal wound, drenching his clothes.

Just then, another scout came riding up and drew back his arm to thrust his lance into Karim Khan's unprotected back, when Khan's aide, Ali, a cheerful-looking young man with a round face, who was just behind that scout, realizing the mortal danger his leader was in, hurled his own lance at the attacker. It grazed the man's right shoulder, which was enough for the lance to drop from his grip.

'What good fun!' exclaimed Ali, exhilarated at the skirmish, a broad smile lighting up his face, his eyes glinting in anticipation of more action, but before he could say anything further, one of the scouts who had remained in the rear and was also armed with a lance, thrust his weapon forward, aiming at Ali's stomach. Just at that moment, Ali happened to swerve his horse, with the result that the vicious tip of the lance missed his stomach but cut itself deep into his upper right thigh. Seeing his colleague thus beset, Karim Khan, who himself had fought off two of the scouts, rode rapidly forward and distracted his colleague's attacker.

By this time, the scouts realized that further resistance was useless and no help was at hand. They threw down their weapons and dismounted, looking sullenly at their captors.

'Tie them up and have them mounted on their horses,' Karim Khan ordered. 'We will take them with us.'

A few of his sowars got down swiftly from their saddles and trussed the scouts up, with their arms behind their backs. Helping them put their foot into the stirrup, their feet were then bound under the girth of their horses to prevent them from falling. The dead man's foot was released from the stirrup and the body was thrown into the nearby bushes. Meanwhile, Karim Khan went towards Ali and helped him off his horse. He carefully exposed the thigh wound by cutting the cloth around it with his dagger. The gaping wound looked wicked, with the flesh all lacerated and blood oozing out. Tearing a strip of cloth from Ali's undershirt, he took the help of another sowar in fashioning a tourniquet, which he tightly tied above the wound to staunch the flow of blood. Then, wetting some sand from his water bottle, he made a mud cake out of it and then applied it to the wound, which he then covered with a bandage. It is for little acts of concern like these for his men, that they were willing to die for him.

'Do you think you can hold out for some time?' he asked Ali.

The gravely wounded young man was in great pain, but he nodded. He was willing to give his life for his commander and he dared not let him down now. He hobbled back to his horse with difficulty, and two of his colleagues helped him mount.

Karim Khan turned to the other sowars. 'Any of you know a place nearby where Ali can be treated?' he asked.

A sowar nodded. 'One of my uncles is a hakeem in Baradih village, which is about three kos from here, Sahib.'

'Good. Here is a gold mohur.' Karim Khan dug into one

of his pockets and fished out a gold coin, which glinted dully by the light of the sickle moon. He threw it across and the sowar plucked it out of the air expertly. 'Take Ali with you and have him treated. Take Sarfaraz with you,' he added, pointing towards a young sowar. 'If the hakeem wants more money, give it and take it from me later, but see that Ali's treatment lacks nothing and he remains with the hakeem there till his wound is fully healed. See that all this is done quietly without causing any commotion in the village. Join us after Ali is placed in the hakeem's hands.'

The two sowars nodded. They wheeled their horses on either side of Ali's own and holding his bridle as he lurched in the saddle, they led him away.

Then riding back to Dara, who, along with the rest of the party, had stopped at some distance to watch the affray, Karim Khan said, 'We will have to hasten our pace, Sire. These scouts from the enemy cavalry detachments can only mean that the detachments themselves are not very far away, and in case they block our path, we will be heavily outnumbered.'

Dara agreed. The carriages were whipped forward, and with the ladies swaying and jolting in them, clinging on to whatever support their interiors could provide, and the men riding alongside, with two squadrons of the cavalry in front and three behind, the party raced forward along the road towards Delhi, raising huge columns of dust into the night air. As they drew away from the fort, the orchards laden with mangoes for the imperial court and the nobility, which nestled right up to the walls of the fort, gave way to open fields now barren, except for the wheat stubble that was baking in the summer heat. Here and there, patches of green could be seen which provided the vegetable produce for the townspeople, while at some distance beyond, lay large groves of forests, dark and forbidding, matted with dense vegetation, and devoid of human habitation, except for the occasional soft-yellow light of a wick lamp that could be seen flickering through the foliage which betokened the presence of a village.

Leaving the massive gate of Sikandra, the resting place of Dara's great ancestor Akbar and his now-deserted capital city of Fatehpur Sikri far behind them, the first light of dawn found the party near a small clearing, past which ran a narrow rivulet. Despite the high summer, there was some water flowing in it and Karim Khan called a halt. They had been riding practically non-stop throughout the night and the heaving flanks of the horses flecked with lather made it clear that they could not go further without a much-needed rest, as replacements for the mounts would not be possible till they reached Delhi. Pickets were posted all round the clearing and as canvas panels were raised to provide privacy to the royal family, Nadira, Jahanzeb and the ladies-in-waiting stepped down from their carriages to stretch their tired limbs.

A short while later, one of Karim Khan's most intrepid couriers, whom he had stationed in Agra ahead of the pursuers to watch and report on the enemy's movements, reached the outermost picket, where he was intercepted and escorted by two sowars. He was brought in to the presence of Karim, who lay stretched out by the side of the rivulet, eyes closed, imagining Saira, with her lovely face and lissome body next to him, his lips pressed against hers and idly wondering whether she had deliberately missed her step to fall into his arms.

'Well, Junaid, what news do you bring? Are the rebel detachments anywhere close by?' asked Karim Khan as the courier discreetly coughed, causing the captain to sit up.

'The pursuit has been deferred for the present, Huzoor,' replied the courier between gasps after he had paused to draw breath. 'The rebels were too exhausted to follow, and many of them were engaged in looting the imperial camp. His Majesty has declared that the gates of Agra Fort will not be opened and all the rebel units have been detailed around the fort to besiege it. The siege guns were being hauled into position at the time I left, in case the fort did not surrender and ladders were being arranged to scale its walls. Cavalry regiments as well as smaller guns of the enemy were being stationed in readiness in front of the fort's gates to thwart any breakout. The fort has been closely invested and all the roads leading out of it have been blockaded.'

'Well, the fact that we are no longer being pursued is the first bit of good news we have heard and we are lucky to have got out in time,' said Dara, a weak smile passing fleetingly over his haggard face when Karim Khan went up to him and reported what he had been told by his courier, Junaid. Then, Dara became serious, 'But we fear for the Emperor. Our abandoned brothers will leave no stone unturned to capture Agra, going so far as to imperil the person of His Majesty and then they will turn on Delhi. Once Agra falls and the Emperor comes into their custody, sooner or later, Aurangzeb will render Murad ineffective and seize the throne. I can see it all happening as clear as daylight and as long as there is breath in my body, I will not let it happen. It is vital that we reach Delhi as soon as possible. How soon can we strike camp and proceed ahead?'

'Sire, the horses are completely exhausted and require rest. Mounts to replace them will not be available and we will have to make do with them for quite some time. It will be safe to halt here for a while before we proceed and, in the meantime, the horses will be rested and watered. As the pursuit has been called off, there is no immediate threat,' replied the tall captain courteously.

'We leave it to your best judgement,' replied Dara kindly. 'You have brought us without mishap up till here and we have no doubt that you will be able to ensure our safety till we reach Delhi. We ourselves are greatly fatigued, and we know that the horses are too, but our principal anxiety is to reach Delhi as soon as possible.'

Karim Khan bowed and withdrew.

Meanwhile, behind the canvas panels that had been raised to ensure privacy, Nadira and the ladies-in-waiting performed their ablutions by the waters of the flowing rivulet and partook of the humble fare that they had brought along with them.

Soon, they were on their way again.

Two

O n the third day of their flight from Agra, as they were approaching the ancient town of Mathura, just as dawn was breaking, a cloud of dust could be discerned moving swiftly towards them. Could it be rebel units? Bidding the party to take whatever cover was possible in a mango grove nearby, Karim Khan, along with a few sowars, went stealthily forward to the edge of the grove to investigate. When he spied the pennants and emblems of the imperial army being carried by the leading horsemen, he breathed a sigh of relief. They were friendly forces. He rode forward and greeted Nawab Dawood Khan.

The Nawab was a mansabdar of two thousand horsemen, short and stocky, who had lost his left eye from a splinter during a Persian artillery barrage, when they had successfully broken the Mughal defence in the siege of Kandahar, six years earlier, but his boast was that his good eye was sufficient to spot and decapitate the head of any enemy. He had been deputed by Shah Jahan to serve under Shuja in Bengal, but when that prince had raised the standard of revolt, Dawood Khan had quitted Shuja's service and had returned to Agra, where he had been made head of the household troops in the battle of Samugarh. He had sworn unswerving fealty to the Emperor and reckoning Dara to be the Emperor's rightful heir, he was among Dara's most loyal followers.

'My Lord Dara is in the grove over there,' said Karim Khan, pointing to the clump of trees as the Nawab's forces rode forward and then mingled with Dara's men with much conviviality and backslapping.

'Welcome, Khan sahib,' said Dara, smilingly, as he extended his right hand, which the Nawab brushed with his lips. 'We understand that Agra Fort has been closely invested, so how were you and your men able to evade the blockade and what is the present situation there?'

Dawood Khan took a little time to draw his breath and then said, 'Luckily, these men whom I have brought with me were well outside the fort precincts when the blockade was ordered, Your Highness. By word of mouth, we secretly assembled in ones and twos in Behrampur village, which is nearly ten kos west of Agra. From there, riding practically non-stop and by a wide circuitous route to evade the rebel patrols, we reached here. Till the time we left, two days ago, His Majesty had refused to open the gates of the fort and the siege has been tightened. Negotiations were underway, Your Highness. The rebel princes have demanded unimpeded access to the fort and have threatened that unless the gates were opened by sunrise this morning, they would commence bombardment, in which case, His Majesty's safety could not be guaranteed. The siege guns are all in position, and they are only waiting for the word.'

'Can the fort hold out?' asked Dara.

'Unlikely, Sire. Not for long at any rate. You would recall that many of the heavy guns which were taken from Agra and positioned along the embankments at Dholpur to prevent the rebels crossing the Chambal River had to be left behind there when they bypassed that spot and some others have been captured by them at Samugarh,' the honest soldier replied.

At the mention of that battle, Dara's face blanched for a second and Karim Khan avoided catching his eye. 'The few small pieces that are left in the fort will be nowhere near enough to knock out the enemy's gun emplacements.'

'All the more reason then that we reach Delhi as soon as possible. What is the strength of the men you have brought along with you?'

'Two hundred, Sire. All cavalry. I wanted to be at My Lord's elbow as soon as possible. About a hundred others including my family have been left inside the fort to make their way out as best they can if and when the situation normalizes.'

Dara was deeply moved by Khan's willingness to disregard even his family's safety to be with him. He stretched out his arms and grasped Dawood Khan's shoulders. Looking at him in the eye, he said, 'We shall never forget this.'

Then, turning to Karim Khan, he said, 'Well, we should make a move now.'

Two days later, as they were passing a khanqah of the celebrated Pir Mian Aatish Bilgrami, on the outskirts of Beawar village, a mendicant staggered out of its courtyard and as Dara rode past, he somehow dodged the guards who were on either side and grabbed at Dara's stirrup.

'Hail, Exalted One!' he cried in a hoarse voice, rattling his rusted iron cup against his wooden staff as he ran alongside Dara's horse. The guards tried to push the man aside, but Dara ordered them to desist. Normally, Dara would not have bothered even to throw a second glance at the man, but something in the man's intense gaze as he looked up at Dara made the prince take a second look at him. He felt that he had seen the man before. The man was dressed in rags, whose tattered edges barely reached down to his dirt-encrusted knees and a soiled turban sat on top of his head below which was a mat of grey hair, and a thin, foxy-looking face covered with a straggly beard and a pair of close-set eyes. When he opened his mouth, it showed rotting teeth.

'May the splendour of a thousand suns light Your Excellency's path. Give this humble creature a few coins, Master, which is but dust in your precious hands, for has it not been said that to give to the needy is the highest form of worship to that one God whom we all call by different names? Give this humble creature a few coins, Master!'

'Here, take this,' Dara said as he reached into his pocket and drew out a gold mohur, which he tossed into the man's cup.

'Allah be praised,' the beggar cried, his face lighting up. 'They are truly generous who see God in every creature, nay in every particle of dust.'

On hearing this line, Dara looked even more intently at the man for it was from one of his own compilations of ghazals and rubaiyats on Sufism and Quadriism.

'For all your poverty-stricken appearance, you seem to be a learned man,' said Dara as he rode forward, the man running after him, clutching his stirrup.

'Do not judge a book by its cover, Your Excellency,' said the beggar.

Dara was beginning to enjoy this verbal jousting. 'We shall be breaking journey for a short rest in that copse of trees that you see in front of you,' he said. 'Perhaps we can learn from each other,' he added.

'Willingly, Your Excellency,' said the mendicant.

Dara signalled to one of his aides to seat the man on a horse and with surprising agility, the man sprang up behind a sowar.

On reaching the clump of trees, a small marquee was raised and pickets were posted all around for Dara to rest.

Dara then sent for the mendicant, who took his seat at Dara's feet.

'Ah, we thought we had seen you before,' smiled Dara as the man removed his disguise, taking the prince's hand and placing it over his head.

He was Bashir Ahmed, one of the most skilful of the confidential agents in Shah Jahan's court, with unrivalled intelligence contacts, who was known to be capable of providing his master with accurate information—whatever the odds.

'Your disguise is certainly very effective. What is the news from Agra? We have been on the road since the last six days and except for the news brought by Nawab Dawood Khan three days after we left Agra, we have been receiving only garbled rumours. We thirst for authentic information.'

'Agra has fallen, Your Highness,' said Ahmed. 'The day after it fell, I hastened from the city in this disguise to report to you. Although the blockade is tight, they did not stop a poor, harmless mendicant like me when I told them I was proceeding to offer namaz at the dargah of Nizamuddin Auliya.' He chuckled and then continued. 'After His Majesty had refused to open the city gates, the fort was surrounded and the siege guns were hauled into position, but in the end, all those preparations were found unnecessary. Somebody suggested to Prince Aurangzeb that it would be far easier to force the city into submission if the water supply from the Jamuna River was cut off, and that is exactly what was done. In this blistering heat, the water available in the fort was sufficient only for three days and, on the fourth day, the fort was compelled to capitulate.'

'And His Majesty? What about him? How are he and Jahanara Begum?' asked Dara, anxiously biting his lip.

'According to last reports, both are well, Sire, but are confined to their palaces within the fort complex under a strong guard. None are allowed to meet them without the permission of Prince Aurangzeb's faithful eunuch Aitbaar, except Roshanara Begum, who hastened her return from Kashmir and reached Agra the day the city fell.'

'Did not the Emperor summon his rebellious sons into his presence and berate them for their contumacy in daring to raise their sword against the throne?' Dara asked. It was essential to know how the Emperor had reacted to the developing situation.

'He did, Your Highness, but they evaded his summons, using every subterfuge, all the while protesting their loyalty towards him. The Emperor, for his part, tried every stratagem in the book—anger, bluster, guile and praise, but without success. He plied them with costly presents and gifts, while inviting them into his presence, even lauding Prince Aurangzeb for being a true Muslim and going so far as to present him with a ceremonial sword. When that did not work either, he tried to play upon Prince Aurangzeb's sympathy remarking that barely a few days ago, he was the master of Hindustan, with nine lakh troops at his beck and call, while now he, a living being, was forced to beg for a cup of water from his sons, when the Hindus offered water even to their dead. That plaintive remark too had no effect, and when it was carried to Prince Aurangzeb, he is believed to have observed to some of the nobles present that all that had come to pass was because of His Majesty's own fault in...er...favouring one prince above the others all along...' Bashir Ahmed uttered these words, and then paused, his head lowered, arms crossed in front of him, not daring to look Dara in the eye, as the reference was directly to Dara himself.

'Go on,' said Dara harshly.

'...and failing to order opening of the gates of Agra Fort, when all that the two brothers wanted was to satisfy themselves that the Emperor was well...'

'..."the emperor was well"...the lying, mendacious, scoundrels,' muttered Dara to himself, repeating Ahmed's words. They were willing to bombard the Emperor's palace only to see that he was well.

'Moreover, there are rumours that Roshanara Begum sent a message warning Prince Aurangzeb not to present himself before the Emperor, as she had overheard some whispers in the harem that His Majesty planned to have him arrested and killed as soon as he entered the royal presence, which is why he adopted every trick known to man to evade obeying the Emperor's summons,' Ahmed added.

Could there be any truth in the rumour? Dara wondered. He knew that the Emperor could be quite ruthless, but murdering his own son? Dara discounted the rumour, attributing it to be one more of his sister's devious moves to sow discord within the family.

'And what about Prince Murad?' he asked.

'Yes, he, too, has joined Prince Aurangzeb.'

'But surely at least he would have opposed such humiliating treatment of the Emperor.'

'We are small beings, Your Highness, and it does not lie in our mouths to comment on such high personages, but Prince Murad has done nothing to intercede in His Majesty's favour,' replied Ahmed, not daring to look up at Dara. 'He remains within his palace in the premises of the fort all day with his string of dancing girls except when he is out hunting and even there, he takes one or two of them to entertain him. It is said that he is particularly enamoured of a Circassian beauty with green eyes, whom he had sent for all the way from Ahmedabad and who accompanies him on his hunts. According to rumours, when he is in his cups, he has been heard boasting to some of his boon companions that now there are only two to rule over the empire of Hindustan, namely himself and Prince Aurangzeb, and he will compel the prince to partition it between the two, in accordance with some understanding they had reached when they joined forces, till such time as the opportunity arises for him to settle accounts finally with Prince Aurangzeb.'

Sons against the father. Brother against brother. A sister bent on creating further wedges in the family—deceit, treachery and intrigue. Will there ever be an end to all of this? wondered Dara distractedly.

'And what of Prince Aurangzeb himself? Any idea of his plans?' he asked after sometime.

'As you know, Your Highness, he is extremely secretive and divulges his plans to none. For the present, he is consolidating his hold in and around Agra. Many of his commanders who distinguished themselves in battle have been presented khillats and jagirs, or their mansabs have been raised and high honours have been conferred upon them. The local rajas and nawabs are falling over themselves in rushing into his presence to pay court to him, while those among the doubters are being tempted with extravagant offers, it being conveyed to them, secretly of course, that the imperial cause in any case is hopeless. Many of the generals whom Prince Sulaiman had taken with him in the conflict against Prince Shuja in the east along with their troops are believed to have defected and have conveyed their allegiance to Prince Aurangzeb, including Mirza Raja Jai Singh of Mewar. In fact, I have it on good authority that when Prince Sulaiman summoned Mirza sahib and Nawab Diler Khan to plan the march on to Agra, they demurred and informed him that as most of his army in any case had fled on hearing of Prince Aurangzeb's victory at Samugarh, it would be in his own best interest to flee lest he was caught. He is believed to have sent an urgent message to Raja Prithvi Chand of Garhwal seeking refuge and is awaiting a reply. Meanwhile, an inventory is being made of the wealth in the vaults of the imperial treasury. The army is being re-equipped and recruitment has been stepped up. The cannon foundries have been ordered to work overtime. It is believed that within a few days, the prince will commence his march on to Delhi.'

Dara was stunned to hear the news. Sulaiman, his son and the vanquisher of his brother Shuja, on whose army he had pinned much of his hopes to set right the balance and restore the Emperor to the throne, now himself a supplicant and that too in the court of an unbeliever? His grandiose plans of leading the attack from the west and Sulaiman from the east now lay shattered. Were all the fates ranged against him in these testing times? No, it could not be true. It must have been only a rumour. Ahmed was probably mistaken.

'Are you absolutely sure of this? About Raja Prithvi Chand being approached for shelter? In fact, before we left Agra, we had written a letter to our son to keep himself in readiness to march on to Agra when we gave the signal and began our advance from Delhi.'

'You know my sources are unimpeachable, Your Highness. Has this humble creature ever let Your Highness down?'

Dara was silent for a while. Now with any assistance from

Sulaiman ruled out at least for the present, it was all the more necessary to reach Delhi as soon as possible and organize the troops there to face the rebels.

'As you know, we are anxious to reach Delhi as soon as possible,' he said after some time. 'Its governor, Nawab Zulfiqar Baksh, owes his life to us. Indeed the Emperor was ready to have him beheaded for slackness in the defence of Kandahar during its siege by the Persians, but it is on our intercession that he was spared and later, much later, even restored to office. We hope he will not create any problems for us.'

'Beware, Your Highness. Pardon my saying so, but on the day he entered Agra, Prince Aurangzeb is believed to have written a letter to Nawab sahib, which was carried by a fast courier, warning him that if he opened Delhi's gates to Your Highness, he and his family would pay for it with their lives. That letter is bound to have reached him by now and it is very unlikely that he will allow your party to enter Delhi. Any amount of gold is unlikely to persuade him to do so, as he would value his and his family's life above everything else for he knows that what Prince Aurangzeb says, he does. Even if he does allow your party to enter, you risk getting trapped inside the fort as the troops with you are far too few in relation to the numbers inside to enable you to fight your way out.'

Dara sat silently for a while digesting all the information that Ahmed had brought him. 'You have given us valuable intelligence,' he said at length. 'It will help us greatly in formulating our future plans. Here, do accept this,' he peeled off a diamond ring that he was wearing and placed it in the agent's palm. 'What are your plans?'

'Your Highness is most gracious,' said Ahmed as he raised the gift to his forehead. 'I will be getting back to Agra as quickly as possible. My family is there and I am worried about their safety in these unsettled times.'

'Khuda Hafiz,' said Dara.

Ahmed bowed and withdrew as Dara watched his retreating figure.

So it had come to this, thought Dara bitterly to himself as he sat alone for a while in the marquee. All this had come to pass because of the mistakes he had committed in the battle of Samugarh which had led to his defeat—his overconfidence, his failure to seize the moment and attack despite the good counsel given to him by his generals to do so when the enemy had reached the battlefield still unready and disorganized; the failure of resolve when his hated brother was within his sights and one last effort would have brought Aurangzeb to his knees; and above all, him alighting from his elephant and taking to a horse on poor advice at the concluding stages of the battle, thereby spreading consternation among his troops at seeing the royal howdah empty and prompting large-scale desertions. That defeat had now led to this state—he and his family, fugitives fleeing for their lives; their father, the Emperor, on whose lap the brothers had once sat in those bygone years, now a prisoner; his son, the pearl of his eye, seeking refuge in a Hindu court; his own entry into the imperial capital of Delhi probably barred for the present; and the Peacock Throne, in all but name, in the hands of a fanatical bigot.

For the rest of the day and late into the night, Dara kept mulling over what his next course of action should be. It was vital to free the Emperor, not only because he was the legitimate ruler of the empire, but to ensure Dara's own succession to the throne, but how? Lead an army from Delhi and hope to reconquer Agra? Even if he secured access to the capital in the absence of steadfast allies, there was little chance of that succeeding, as the garrison there was sorely depleted, with the best generals, along with the bulk of its forces there, having been lost at Samugarh. Rally the great Rajput and Jat feudatories to the imperial cause? After Jai Singh's defection, all the others, barring a couple, would most likely prefer to wait and watch the situation to see which side would emerge triumphant before pledging their swords. Proceed to Lahore and organize the forces there to attack Aurangzeb's strongholds, while Shuja was coaxed to mount a diversionary assault from the east, so as to split the rebel forces with the promise of a great viceroyalty? Yes, perhaps that was a more feasible proposition and some possibilities opened out there, but would Shuja accept the offer when he nursed imperial ambitions himself, and more particularly when he had been beaten by Dara's own son? And would not all this take months when time was of the essence, and with each hour that passed, Aurangzeb consolidated his grip?

Dara kept these thoughts to himself and shared the information given by Ahmed to him with none. He did not want to alarm Nadira unnecessarily and mentioning it to Dawood Khan risked the information even unwittingly spreading to others, leading to defection among the few troops he had brought with him, on their assuming that the imperial cause was lost. Moreover, there was still a glimmer of hope that Bashir Ahmed's information might not be correct and Zulfiqar Baksh would open the gates of Delhi for them.

Thus after hastening their pace when they finally came within sight of the tall column of the Qutub Minar away in the distance to their left and a little later, the brooding battlements of the now-deserted Tughlaqabad Fort to their right, Dara put on a brave face and pretended to rejoice with the others.

'Look, Mother, the Qutub Minar,' cried Jahanzeb excitedly as she peered through a chink in the curtains of her carriage.

'Allah be praised,' exclaimed Nadira, clasping her daughter tightly to herself in the jolting carriage as she closed her eyes and fervently murmured a prayer. At long last, the safety of the outer fort walls of Delhi; the security of the Red Fort within those outer walls; an escape from the clouds of dust and the enervating heat that sat like a huge boulder on their shoulders; the comforts of the royal palace with a hammam for a much-needed bath; clean clothes to wear, fresh food to eat and ice-cold water to drink. She parted the curtains of the carriage a little bit and looked at Dara and Siphir, who were riding by her side, with Dawood Khan a little behind. 'Delhi,' she said, pointing in the direction of the imperial capital. 'At last.'

Dara smiled and nodded. Delhi was near!

Passing through the narrow pathways in the Jahanpanah forest, which was the royal hunting preserve, and skirting the great white dome of Emperor Humayun's tomb and then picking their way through the cenotaphs and mausoleums that marked the resting place of the Lodi kings, the party at length arrived at a plain, interspersed with trees and orchards belonging to the crown and the nobility through which the massive dun-coloured sandstone walls of Delhi Fort, recently renovated by Shah Jahan, could be seen shimmering in the noon day heat—as if in a mirage. The party halted at the edge of the plain, while Dawood Khan rode ahead with a handful of sowars up to the southern gate of the city and when he was within a bow shot of it, he signalled to his sowars to rein in their steeds.

'Open in the name of the Emperor of Hindustan,' he cried.

He could clearly see the lookouts on the ramparts of the fort, talking excitedly among themselves, but no attempt was made to open the gates. Then, a single musket shot rang out which kicked the dirt around Dawood Khan's horse's hooves.

'I say open,' Dawood Khan cried again. 'Prince Dara, the Wali Ahad, commands entry. Have you not received the Emperor's firman that the Wali Ahad has to be given the same facilities as given to the Emperor? By heaven, if you delay any further and the Emperor gets to hear of this, you shall be flogged within an inch of your lives.'

Even that cry evoked no movement to open the gates. Then Dawood Khan saw the snout of a cannon glinting wickedly in the sunlight as it was pushed through an embrasure in the fort walls. There was a puff of smoke and a cannonball whistled over their heads and ploughed into some sand behind them just as the sound of a cannon being fired reverberated in their ears. Had the fort gone over to the rebels? There was only one way to find out.

Dawood Khan rode back to where the rest of the party had halted. 'The guards refuse to open the gates and we do not have the wherewithal to compel them to open it,' he said as he drew near Dara. 'Perhaps if Your Highness showed himself to them, they might relent.'

'Very well,' replied Dara as he spurred his horse forward and escorted by Nawab Dawood Khan, Karim Khan and the squadrons of cavalry he approached the gate of the fort.

'Here is the Wali Ahad in person before you,' shouted Dawood Khan. 'He bids you to open the gate for him to enter.'

At the sight of Dara, along with Dawood Khan and the cavalry squadrons behind them, further hectic confabulations could be seen taking place along the ramparts of the fort. A stout, important-looking personage could be spotted peering through an embrasure above the gate and then nodding. After a brief while, the bolts in the wicket gate could be heard turning and the deputy governor of the fort along with a few officials and troopers scurried across the intervening land up to Dara.

'A thousand apologies, Your Highness,' said Mukhtar Gul, the deputy governor, sweating profusely as he kissed Dara's stirrup. 'But I have strict instructions from Nawab Zulfiqar Baksh not to open the gates.' Then to explain Baksh's absence, he added, 'The Nawab is ill today with colic and is unable to be present in person.'

'What arrant nonsense is this?' Dawood Khan roared. 'Don't you see who is before you? It is the Wali Ahad, the heir to the throne of Hindustan. Are you going to allow him to wait here in the heat? By Allah, if the Emperor gets to hear of this, he will have you flayed alive.'

'Those are my orders, Your Excellency,' replied Gul doggedly, making no move to have the gates opened.

To avoid causing Dara any further embarrassment, Dawood Khan suggested that Dara retire to the orchard to their rear where, to escape the heat the others were waiting, while he sorted out the matter with the governor. Dara nodded forlornly and turned the head of his horse round towards the orchard. Ahmed's information was proving tragically correct.

'Take me to the governor,' Dawood Khan ordered with as much authority as he could muster. Somehow, he felt he was fighting a lost battle.

'Very well, but you will have to come alone and unarmed,' replied Gul.

Dawood Khan unbuckled his sword and handed it over

to a sowar standing nearby. He then followed Gul across the intervening land, through the wicket gate and into the fort.

Meanwhile, sitting in her carriage, Nadira visualized the great gates of the fort swinging open for them to enter and the few onlookers standing just within it in the torrid heat of that afternoon, bowing low and then straightening up to raise their arms high in the air seeking the royal benediction, crying *'Anna data, Anna data'* as they always did when they recognized Dara. In her mind's eye, she saw the party sweeping past the gate flanked by the cavalrymen, going up the broad road that passed through the aristocratic quarter of Daryaganj, with the palaces of the nobility and the various embassies to the Mughal court on either side, which then opened out onto a wide foreground. Crossing the foreground with the colossal edifice of the Jama Masjid on its enormous plinth to the left; and at the point where it intersected Chandni Chowk, with the waters of the Nahr-e-Bahisht flowing through its middle, now reduced to a trickle in high summer, she could visalize the party wheeling right towards the massive Lahori gate of the Red Fort, with its seven arched domes, a minaret at either end and flanked by a big tower on either side. Then clattering across the cobblestones of the Meena Bazaar, the long, covered arcade lined with shops and coffee houses and then entering the forecourt of the Red Fort with a reflecting pool in the centre before reaching their palace in the northern precincts of the fort.

However, when the sun, which was high on the meridian at the time they had arrived at the Delhi gate, had by now dipped perceptibly towards the south-west, and the gate had still not opened, her temper began to fray.

'Ask your father what is holding the opening of the gate

up,' Nadira said to Siphir. 'How long are we going to sit here and get roasted?'

Siphir went up to Dara and put the question to him, upon which Dara rode up to Nadira's carriage.

'Just a little while longer,' he pleaded. 'There seems to be some mix-up. Nawab Dawood Khan has gone to sort out the matter.' He was loathe to tell her about Ahmed's warning, which was becoming increasingly true with each passing moment.

At length, Dawood Khan emerged out of the fort. His face was drawn. As the others watched, he crossed the length of the ground to the orchard where Dara and the others were waiting. Drawing Dara aside, he whispered in his ear, 'The governor has refused to open the gates under any circumstance, Your Highness. He says that if he opens the gates, he has been warned by Prince Aurangzeb that neither he nor his family members, who are presently in Agra, will live to see the next sunrise. I tried everything—threats, warnings, appeals to his good sense, gold, but he has totally refused, so great is his fear of Prince Aurangzeb. He says that it is only because you saved him from the Emperor's wrath that he has not sent his troops to arrest us, knowing that we are no match for their numbers.'

'It is just as we feared. Aurangzeb has beaten us to it. What do you suggest we do now?' Dara mumbled, despair clutching his heart.

'Our best hope is to proceed as quickly as we can to Lahore, Your Highness.'

When Nadira received the news from Dara that Delhi's gates were closed and the only alternative was to move to Lahore, she was flabbergasted. 'What? Proceed to Lahore? But we have just arrived here in Delhi. How can they close its gates on us?' she remonstrated. 'Do you realize what this means? It will take at least three weeks to reach Lahore even if all goes well, right through the worst part of summer. Siphir's wound is still to heal and you know how ill Jahanzeb has been throughout the journey, from Agra till here. I am just not moving out from here, come what may.'

'Try and understand,' replied Dara pleadingly. 'Zulfiqar Baksh has been warned by Aurangzeb that if he opens the gates for us, his entire family, who are in Agra, will be executed. Our numbers are pitiful compared with the troops inside the fort, and moreover we have no artillery to break down its walls. Aurangzeb is bound to come after us and we just cannot fight him anywhere near Delhi without troops and military wherewithal. Our only hope of defeating Aurangzeb and rescuing the Emperor is to proceed to Lahore and make a stand somewhere in its vicinity. The troops there are sufficient in number and fresh, and the garrison is adequately stocked with war material. Additional troops can also be requisitioned from Kabul should the need arise. By the time the enemy reaches us there, the rains would have broken, and the Sutlej River, swollen with the monsoon rains, will prove to be an impassable barrier for their heavy guns.'

'You go to Lahore or wherever else you want to go,' replied Nadira rebelliously. 'If Sulaiman is able to join you, all the better, and both of you can tackle your brothers. Siphir and Jahanzeb will stay here with me. Your brothers may have a quarrel with you, but surely Aurangzeb will respect me.' Then drawing herself up, she said proudly. 'Let him not forget that I am a Mughal princess and like in him, in my veins too flows the blood of the emperors Akbar and Jahangir. If I remind

Aurangzeb of that, I am confident that he will allow the children and me to live here in peace.'

'Perish the thought,' scoffed Dara with asperity in his voice. 'Reminding him of your common ancestry and allowing you and the children to live there in peace? Indeed! Have you no idea by now what the man is really made of? If he can imprison his own father and sister and make his elder brother a fugitive, he can be up to anything. If you and the children fall into his clutches, he will most likely make use of all of you as hostages to get me to surrender, and once he succeeds in doing that, your life and that of the children will be of no consequence to him.'

'But leaving Delhi, just after we have reached here?' Nadira wailed. 'Another journey in this heat? A journey which may take anywhere up to three weeks, with bad food and little water, no proper place to rest or bathe or even change one's clothes? And what is the guarantee that we will not have to flee from Lahore too?'

'Nobody can give any guarantee, but that is our only chance,' replied Dara brusquely. Then he softened. Grasping Nadira by the shoulders and looking down into her eyes, he added, 'Remember, we have to stay together and support each other if we are to come out of this ordeal successfully. We will make the journey in much easier stages than when we had to leave Agra. Moreover, there are several resting places where we can halt on the way. Meanwhile, Siphir's wound will also heal and Jahanzeb hopefully will recover fully, provided she strictly follows the treatment prescribed by hakeem sahib, which you must ensure that she does.'

'What about Sulaiman? You mentioned some plan of his attacking from the east, while you attacked from the west.

Even if the troops in Delhi are not with us, surely he can attack the rebels?'

Dara did not want to tell her that many of Sulaiman's best generals and troops had defected and he himself was seeking shelter in the court of a Hindu prince, as the news would probably be too much for her to bear at this point.

'Er…yes, but he would require support and that can be provided only if we proceed as quickly as possible to Lahore and organize the troops there. Then we will be able to attack Aurangzeb from two sides, we from the north-west and Sulaiman from the east.'

As Dara drew Nadira into his arms and pressed her head against his chest, she nodded resignedly, realizing that there was no point in taking the argument any further. Dara's mind was made up, and truly, there seemed to be no alternative except to accompany him to Lahore and wherever else he chose to take her, but somehow, the premonition was growing inside her that this would not be the end of their flight.

Three

Ten days after making his victorious entry into Agra, confining his father and sister in their apartments overlooking the Taj Mahal with strict orders that they were to lack nothing except their liberty, and having tidied up affairs in the city and its vicinity, Aurangzeb got ready to march on to Delhi. He had sent one of his senior commanders, Nasri Khan, who had switched sides and pledged his loyalty to Aurangzeb, in pursuit of Dara two days earlier. Nasri Khan had assured his new master that he would bring the head of that hapless prince swinging from his saddlebags. Shuja was still licking his wounds after the defeat he had suffered at the hands of Sulaiman near Benares, and Sulaiman himself was now on the run after the defections of Jai Singh, Diler Khan and many of his other leading generals. Thus, things were panning out favourably for Aurangzeb and he had reasons to be pleased with himself. The only immediate impediment to his sole writ running across the heartland of Hindustan was his brother Murad and he felt the time had come to remove that thorn.

The preparations for the march on to Delhi were elaborate, as Aurangzeb was determined to display to the world the full panoply of Mughal splendour, with himself as its supreme arbiter, and nothing was left to chance. Thus, the night before the march, as was the time-honoured custom, a brace of trumpets were sounded to announce that the march would commence at sunrise the next day, which had been declared to be the most propitious by the court astrologers for a journey in the north-western direction. With the sounding of the trumpets, one set of royal tents, laden on the backs of elephants and camels, proceeded ahead to set up camp at the first halting place, while another set was to move with Aurangzeb's immediate entourage. Together with the first set of tents went some of the heavy artillery pieces with their accompanying gun crew, gunpowder and ball for use should the need arise, drawn by draught oxen as well as the royal kitchen, with cooks, masalchis and khansamas, each responsible for preparing a single dish, along with provisions and condiments of every description and cows to supply fresh milk. Along with them trudged scores of labourers armed with pickaxes, shovels, spades and knives to smoothen the way, with their officers mounted on horseback, wearing badges to signify their rank. Then, as dawn broke, Aurangzeb, seated on a towering, spectacularly caparisoned Ceylonese elephant, with his generals astride their horses on his side, reviewed his troops on the plain abutting the fort before they set off, under the gaze of the people of Agra who had gathered since the early hours to watch the splendid spectacle. To his right were the commanders of the cavalry regiments, each with burnished sword, shield and lance, glinting in the morning sunlight. Their mounts, now and then pawing the hard ground or chomping at the bit as their riders tried to control them. Behind them were the heads of the battalions of musketeers, bowmen, foot soldiers, spear bearers and rocket launchers, including the veterans whom he had brought with him from the Deccan, each in their distinctive gear. To Aurangzeb's left were the elephant and camel corps drawn up in serried ranks interspersed with units of the light artillery that would be hauled by mules. In front were the bannermen, flagbearers, holders of Aurangzeb's personal insignia, drummers, trumpeters, pipers, and flute and shehnai players, while directly behind them were the levies furnished by the feudatories of the region, many of them men of lesser caste, with little or no training, recruited at short notice in response to Aurangzeb's firman. Aurangzeb was aware that barring the hard-bitten Deccan veterans, the household troops and a few other contingents, what had impelled most of the other levies was not so much the bonds of loyalty towards him but the prospect of loot. At the first signs of reverses on the battlefield, or deprived of the chances to plunder, they would desert and run. Yet, overall, their numbers were impressive and would be far more than what Dara would ever be able to range against him.

As his generals closed in around him, with the great kettle drums beating and the trumpets blaring, the army, led by Aurangzeb, streamed out of the plain towards Delhi together with the entire paraphernalia that accompanied a Mughal prince on the move. Ahead rode the generals who would participate in the battle, followed by the bulk of the cavalry, artillery and infantry regiments, behind which came a string of camels laden with gold mohurs, silver rupees, jewellery and precious stones, scoured from the vaults of the Agra treasury and guarded by men fanatically loyal to Aurangzeb to be used to pay adherents to Aurangzeb's cause. They were followed by the royal elephants and horses bearing Aurangzeb's personal flags and standards, behind whom was Aurangzeb himself, followed by his favourite son, Sultan Muhammad, each on his elephant, who were flanked by court officials, ready to furnish details of the territory through which they were passing. Behind them came the scribes and keepers of the official records, and then the ladies of the court similarly seated in covered howdahs, on elephants, while the remaining units of the cavalry and infantry brought up the rear.

As the army debouched from the plain onto the road leading to Delhi, a rider could be seen spurring his horse forward at a furious gallop. He skirted the great throng strung along the road, and dodging the trees and other obstructions on his path, tried to force himself to the front.

'I have...a message for...His Highness. I have been... instructed to deliver it...in person,' he panted as two sturdy guards at length barred his further progress by the points of their crossed lances, while a third held his foam-flecked horse by its bridle. Forcing him to dismount, they held him by the arms, one on either side and parting through the troops that surrounded Aurangzeb, marched him to a court official who was riding by the prince's side.

The courier reached into his tunic and drew out a roll of paper stained with perspiration, which he handed over to the official who, in turn, reached up and passed it onto a guard seated on the elephant behind Aurangzeb.

The guard broke the seal, unrolled the paper and with a bow handed it over to Aurangzeb, who ran his eye over it. The message, which was from one of his confidential agents stationed in Delhi and had been despatched three days earlier, stated that Zulfiqar Baksh had denied access to Dara's party in Delhi and the party was now heading towards Lahore. Apart from the members of Dara's immediate party, the number of accompanying troops was placed at around three hundred. The message also stated that Dara had sent a letter to Nawab

Ifthikar Khan, the governor of Kabul, to send as many troops as he could along with war material to Lahore to reinforce the garrison there for the coming battle with the rebels.

Aurangzeb's eyes gleamed and his lips creased in a wolfish smile. The news was better than ever. Anticipating Dara's likely moves, he had already sent a letter that was despatched by a fast courier to Ifthikar Khan to deny Dara any help that he might seek, and he was sure that Ifthikar would comply, for the governor's dearly beloved niece was one of the princesses in Aurangzeb's harem and he surely would not like anything untoward happening to her. As for the governor of Lahore, Nasri Khan would be sufficient to deal with him, and Dara would be run down to earth sooner than later. Now to deal with Murad, who had proceeded on a tiger hunt and was camping in the forests near Mathura.

Meanwhile, Dara and his party were proceeding towards Lahore.

'The cottage of Alima Mooltani is barely three kos from here,' said Mubarak Beg, one of the officials who was familiar with the area and who happened to be riding by Dara's side, late one afternoon, fifteen days after they had left Delhi. They had crossed the town of Sirhind, which was on the Delhi–Lahore Highway and was the seat of the Mughal provincial administration. He pointed in a westerly direction towards the habitation of the famous pir, knowing Dara's keenness to seek out savants of different faiths.

'Is that so?' exclaimed Dara eagerly. 'How we would like to sit at her feet and invoke her blessing. Do you think that it could be arranged for her to receive us? There will be only my immediate family and me. Of course, we would not like to cause any disruption in her daily routine. We had the good fortune of receiving her blessings once, when we had accompanied the Emperor to Lahore and now that we are so close to where she resides, nothing for us would be more rewarding than to seek her blessings once again.'

'I shall try, Your Highness,' said the official as he spurred his horse towards Alima Mooltani's cottage.

Some time later, he returned, 'Alima would be happy to receive Your Highness, the Begum sahiba and the two children at sundown today,' he said.

Leaving the rest of the party behind, well before sundown that evening, Dara, together with his family members, proceeded towards the cottage of the Alima, which was set in a grove of mango trees. He and Siphir rode horses, while Nadira and Jahanzeb were seated in palanquins. Leaving their mounts and the palanquins some distance from the grove, the four of them trod the narrow path barefoot that led to the mud and thatched hut set in the middle of the grove where the Alima resided.

She received them seated outside her hut under a mango tree, tall and thin, with a long, fair-complexioned face, which still held traces of great beauty, but whose skin, through the ravages of time and the relentless practise of austerities, was now like wrinkled parchment. Thick grey tresses fell away onto her shoulders, and onto the robe she was wearing, but what was most noticeable about her were her piercing eyes, which were hazel in colour, with enormous irises and seemed to penetrate deep into one's soul. An aquiline nose set over a firm mouth completed the visage of this remarkable woman.

As Dara and his family members bowed low before her, touched her feet and then took their seats on the straw mat in front of her, Alima Mooltani looked at them, nodded in acknowledgement, with a slight smile playing on her lips, and then closing her eyes, she began reciting verses from the Holy Koran in praise of Allah, the most Gracious, the most Merciful, and the Cherisher and Sustainer of the Worlds.

At length, she opened her eyes as if she was coming out of a trance, and then looking steadily at Dara, she said, 'I see that deep in your heart, there is something that greatly distresses you. Could I, insignificant though I am, in any way help lighten your burden?'

'Mohtarma, what can be hidden from thou, who knowest all?' replied Dara, in a low monotone with quivering lips, as the cloak of self-confidence that he had donned to hide his insecurities, when he entered her presence, now lay in tatters, for it was clear that she had discerned his innermost thoughts.

'Gone is that day when the Emperor, in his full effulgence, along with this humble self, had entered your gracious presence to receive your blessings. The last few months have seen this ill-fated creature being delivered a series of blows, each more severe than the other, which cumulatively can hardly be endured by mortal man. Treachery and perfidy undid the imperial armies which were forced to suffer two major reverses. The Emperor is now my brother Aurangzeb's prisoner in Agra. My family and I have been locked out of our capital and forced to flee. We are now fugitives in our own land and are being pursued by him whom I shudder to call my brother. We hope to make a stand at Lahore, but our efforts will succeed only if noble souls like yourself intercede with the All Highest so that triumph, justice and righteousness prevail. Pray for us, O Pious One, and give us your guidance for we place our fate in your hands as we don't know which way to turn.'

Alima Mooltani was silent for a long while looking at Dara with kindness in her eyes. Then she spoke, 'Fate ultimately is in the hands of the Great Dispenser, and what is written by him on his Tablets cannot be erased or altered by mere mortals like us. Whatever reverses you might face, your fate will be to reign over the hearts of men of all communities in this vast and varied land in your quest to seek common ground in different religions, while that of your brother is to conquer territories by shedding torrents of blood with the force of arms. Yes, he may wear the crown and wield the sceptre for a while, but that will end with his lifetime, but you, Dara, will live in the annals of Mughal history and be remembered till the end of time as the Prince of Peace. Nothing can take that away from you. Each of us has to fulfil our destiny and yours is to continue to keep searching for those unifying and timeless religious principles that has eluded man down the ages through all the trials and tribulations you might face. Your search may not succeed, but the glory is in the effort. What can be a grander destiny than that? Go now. I have said all that has welled in my heart. May God give you courage and light your path and that of your family's in the coming days.'

Saying that, she dipped her hand into a small bowl that was placed by her side and drew out some marigold flowers and some rose petals, which she extended to Dara and Nadira. They accepted it with both hands and then raised it to their lips and forehead.

Touching the Alima's feet again, Dara and his family members stood up.

'We are indeed blessed to receive these words of divine wisdom, Your Holiness,' replied Dara with folded hands. 'We know not what fate has in store for us, but come what may, we shall continue to face the future with confidence and tread the path we have chosen. In doing so, we will be fortified by your benediction. Permit us to take your leave.'

As Dara and his family bowed before Alima Mooltani, took a few steps backward and then turned and walked away, a strange calm seemed to descend on Dara, but it was Nadira who grasped the portents of Alima Mooltani's message correctly. There would be no safe return for Dara as the heir to the empire in Hindustan. Whatever renown he may gain in the future, that would be in the realm of the spirit. For the present, his fate would be stark and brutal—only exile and at the end, possible death at the hands of his brother.

'What did she mean when she said that Uncle Aurangzeb's destiny is to wear the crown? Will not in good time Abbu be king?' young Jahanzeb asked innocently when they were some distance away from the grove.

'Sssshhh, child,' whispered Nadira. 'Of course, your father will wear the crown.'

As Dara and his family joined the others, a rider came rushing up. He was one of Bashir Ahmed's men and brushing aside the guards who were surrounding Dara, he practically threw himself forward. He indicated that he wanted to convey his message in confidence to Dara alone, who drew him aside, out of hearing of the others.

'I have...ridden from Rupnagar...near Mathura...stopping only to...change horses, Your Highness...Prince Aurangzeb... Delhi...camping at Rupnagar...Prince Murad...' the man gasped incoherently and then stopped to catch his breath.

'Take your time,' said Dara kindly. 'There is no hurry.'

After some time when the man had regained his breath, he continued, 'Prince Aurangzeb is on his way with a large army to Delhi, and has sent Nawab Nasri Khan ahead, while he himself is camping in Rupnagar near Mathura. Meanwhile,

Prince Murad had left Agra earlier for a tiger hunt in those forests. Murad wanted to meet Aurangzeb and discuss the future administration of the empire and its possible partition between the two, with Murad ruling in the west and Aurangzeb in the east.'

'What! Partitioning the empire when the Emperor is still alive. Have they become mad after their victory at Samugarh?' Dara exploded.

The man waited for Dara to regain his composure, and then continued, 'Prince Aurangzeb invited his brother over to his camp for discussions, but used a beautiful slave girl to get him thoroughly drunk and then had him arrested for the murder of Ali Naqvi in Ahmedabad, last year.'

'Yes. We recall that murder. We had persuaded the Emperor to send Naqvi as diwan to straighten out the finances in Gujarat, where Murad is viceroy and our brother murdered him with his own hands in cold blood in the presence of witnesses. So, the two rebels have fallen out. We expected it but not so soon.'

'True, Your Highness. Naqvi's son demanded the head of the murderer in accordance with our laws, and the arrest was made in full view of the nobles accompanying Prince Aurangzeb. Murad was led away in golden fetters. He could not resist, as the few guards he had brought with him had been disarmed. For the present, he is to remain in custody in the fort at Salimgarh, and is later to be removed to the dungeons of Gwalior Fort, where he is to be tried by a court of qazis.

The son was probably instigated by Aurangzeb himself, mused Dara silently, fully conscious of his brother's nature.

That was the end of Murad. He would never get out alive, and next would be Dara's own turn.

'You mentioned Nasri Khan?'

'Yes, Your Highness. He had been sent ahead to Delhi accompanied by a large army by Prince Aurangzeb two days before the prince himself set out from Agra. Nasri Khan has been given strict instructions to capture Your Highness and your party as soon as possible.'

'Where is Nasri Khan now?'

'Roughly midway between Mathura and Delhi. As he is carrying heavy guns with him, his progress is slow. It will take him about seven to eight days to reach Delhi.'

Dara made a quick calculation. Seven days to Delhi and another fortnight for Nasri Khan to reach where he and his party were now. They had a head start of about three weeks, but Lahore was still ten days' journey away and, in case Nasri Khan unleashed his flying columns, that head start could be made up in no time. Moreover, in between lay the broad Sutlej River, which had to be crossed before reaching Lahore, which lay to its north. They would have to hurry. *Would to God that Ifthikar Khan had despatched his troops from Kabul.*

The rains were early that year, and a week after their audience with Alima Mooltani, when Dara, with his small force, had reached the Sutlej, they found that flash floods had made the river swell far beyond its banks, making their crossing extremely hazardous. Indeed, so wide was the river that the opposite bank was barely visible. Yet, cross they had to, for Nasri Khan was hard on their tail, and was now only a week's march behind them. Standing on the lip of the river, under grey skies, with the rain pelting down in sheets, and with the swirling waters of the river submerging all but the tops of the tallest trees, Dara turned to one of his aides, Abdul Majid and gloomily asked, 'How do we get across?'

'We will have to wait till the floods subside, Your Highness,' he replied.

'But that may take days, if not weeks,' Dara retorted. 'We just can't sit here waiting for the water level in the river to recede. Remember, we have to get to Lahore as quickly as possible and shore up its defences against a possible attack. Nasri Khan is now hot on our heels, barely a few days' march away from us, and behind him is Prince Aurangzeb. If we keep sitting here, we might have to fight them with our backs to the river, and that too only with the force we have with us here. We will be wiped out within the hour.'

By this time, a motley collection of around a thousand troops, led by the jagirdars and thikanedars of the territories through which the party was passing, had flocked to Dara's standards, some out of lingering loyalty and respect for the Emperor, but others mainly motivated by the desire to loot and plunder.

'Some of the cavalry and infantry units may get across, but the elephants will refuse to enter the water, and it will be extremely risky for the ladies,' replied Majid, wiping the rain water that had seeped through his umbrella and was streaming down his face.

'Find out about the availability of boats. Surely some boats should be available from the neighbouring villages, which the people use to get across the river. We can assure the boatmen that we will pay handsomely for their services. At least, the ladies and many of the troops will be able to get across. The animals and the equipment can be taken to a spot along the river where it is easier to cross.'

'I had made some inquiries, Your Highness, but as you would have noticed, this tract through which we have been passing is sparsely populated and it is unlikely that there will be anywhere near a sufficient number of boats to get a force as large as ours to cross. The boats in this area are flimsy affairs, which can seat barely five or six persons at a time and will sink as soon as something really heavy is loaded onto them.'

'Well, find out what can be done for us to get across the river. We cannot just sit here waiting for the river to subside.'

'Very well, Your Highness,' replied Majid as he turned the bridle of his horse towards the nearest village and dug his spurs into its flanks.

One watch later, he returned as Dara was about to lose his patience. 'There are only around half-a-dozen boats within a radius of ten kos from here,' he reported. 'The villagers say that since generations, there has been a feud between those living on this bank and those on the other side and neither side crosses the river. It seems that a nawab from across the river carried away a girl belonging to the unbelievers from this side and since then, there has been little or no crossing of the river anywhere near here. However, they can supply some inflatable skins made of buffalo hide, which are lashed together, on which the villagers venture out, but they say it is extremely dangerous to think of crossing the river on those skins in these high floods.'

'Get hold of the boats and the skins along with the boatmen. Tell them we will pay each boatman five gold mohurs to take us across and a gold mohur for each inflatable skin, but if any persons resists, he should be beheaded on the spot. Make an example of one or two of them, and the others are sure to come around,' said Dara. Like many weak men, he, too, was anxious to make a display of his authority.

Soon, the boats were procured and the inflatable water

skins were commandeered on promises mixed with dire threats. In addition, parties of labourers were sent out to cut down some of the sal and sheesham tees that grew some distance away from the bank and were dragged to the spot where the party was waiting and then were lashed together with rope to make them into crude rafts. Karim Khan was chosen to guide the boatmen in the second boat in which sat Nadira, Jahanzeb, Saira and the slave girls, while the lead boat was occupied by Dara, Dawood Khan, Siphir and some of Dara's senior officers. The others in Dara's entourage tried to make themselves as comfortable as possible in the other boats, while the men took to the rafts and the water skins. The elephants and horses were led up the swollen river in search of a spot that would make the crossing easier, where nose to tail they would be led into the water.

It was late in the afternoon of the second day since Dara and his party had reached the swollen Sutlej River by the time the boats were launched into the water, and they were swept along, slowly at first, under the lowering skies as the boatman hugged the riverbank, but to avoid the weeds and reeds that lined it. Karim Khan's head boatman, more venturesome than the others, steered further into the river.

'Be careful,' warned Karim Khan as the boat kept gathering speed, as it was being swept towards the middle of the river, where the current was the swiftest. Suddenly, the boatmen lost control. The boat got caught in a swirling whirlpool and it kept bobbing and spinning round as it was being propelled with an ever-increasing rapidity forward. Soon, Karim Khan and the others found themselves approaching the strong currents in the middle of the river.

Suddenly, the boat dashed itself against a log of wood that

had been swept along in the fast-flowing current. Saira, who sat huddled on the edge of the boat holding onto the oar rest for dear life, lost her grip and was thrown into the water.

'Save me, save me,' she cried as Karim Khan saw her bobbing in the foam-flecked current, with her voluminous burka all that was visible.

'Save her,' cried Nadira as she saw Saira being swept away and the distance between the girl and the boat kept lengthening with every passing moment. 'For the sake of Allah, please save her.'

Without a moment's hesitation, Karim Khan stood up in the boat, and swiftly laying aside his sword, he dived into the swirling waters. Battling the current with powerful strokes, he reached up to where Saira, by now motionless, was floating her hair all undone and visible underneath the burka. With every moment that passed, the distance between Karim Khan and the boat was increasing as they were being swept away from each other.

'Hold my arm,' he cried as he stretched out his hand to grasp her forearm, but there was no response. He realized that he had to do something, and fast.

Positioning himself below Saira and holding her head in both his hands around the ears so that it was kept out of the water, he propelled the two of them with powerful leg strokes towards an outcrop of land in the middle of the riverbed, some distance from where they presently were, which was surmounted by some trees, whose trunks were visible above the river and whose branches were swaying in the wind as the waters lapped its roots. Karim Khan knew that unless they were able to reach the outcrop which would check the speed of their drift on the swift-flowing river, both were done for, as land was not visible on either side of the riverbank as far as the eye could see and Nadira's boat itself was becoming increasingly distant.

With a crash, the force of the current hurled Karim Khan and Saira against the outcrop. With one hand, he held the girl, while with the other, he frantically grabbed at the root of one of the trees which was just visible beneath the swirling waters. Miraculously, his grip held and finding purchase with his feet against the base of the outcrop, he dragged himself and Saira onto its crest, which was barely a hand span above the waves of the river and he came to rest against the trunk of one of the trees.

For the moment, they were safe, but Karim Khan knew that the respite was only momentary. It was now getting dark and although the rains showed some signs of abating, he was aware that were there to be a surge owing to heavy rainfall upstream, there was a strong chance that it would overtop the outcrop, in which case, they would be swept down the river.

Karim looked at Saira. The first thing to do was to revive her. Her eyes were closed, but he noticed the gentle rising and falling of her bosom. *Thank God she is still alive.* But it was clear that she had swallowed a lot of water, which had to be brought out.

Making her sit up and bend forward, he thumped her hard on her back and saw that some of the water she had swallowed was oozing out from her lips. Two or three times he did that and then remembered how as a boy during the flood season, while he and his cousins were swimming in the Jamuna River, one of them had got caught in the current and had nearly drowned whereupon their uncle, who was watching close by, had made the boy lie on his back and had then continued to press his stomach and chest till he had regurgitated most of the water he had swallowed. Then, the uncle had pressed his lips to the boy's mouth and blown hard till the boy had suddenly sat up.

Should he do that to Saira? A natural delicacy at touching the body of the girl made Karim Khan hesitate, but then he reasoned that this was no time to be squeamish. It was not known whether at all a search would be made for them, as it would quite likely be surmised that they had been swept away by the fast-flowing current. Meanwhile, he could not just sit by and watch the life of this beautiful girl ebb away. He removed the sopping wet burka that cloaked her body and saw that beneath it that she wore a salwar-kameez. Placing her on her back, he pressed her waist and bosom with strong upward strokes and noticed that some of the water was trickling through the side of her mouth. Dabbing it with his handkerchief, he put his mouth against hers and blew hard. He felt her petal soft lips quivering against his mouth. He continued to do this for a while and then he saw her eyes fluttering open.

Finding Karim Khan's lean, hard face against hers, she recoiled in embarrassment, 'Where...where...am I?' she muttered.

'You fell out of the boat. I had to dive in to rescue you,' replied Karim Khan, smilingly as he raised his head and sat up. 'Don't worry. We are on a small outcrop in the middle of the river and are safe for the present, unless the water rises sharply, which is unlikely to happen, as the skies seem to be clearing up. People are bound to come looking for us as soon as it is daylight, and till then, we shall have to make ourselves as comfortable as possible. Sorry, I had to get the water you had swallowed out of your system, as otherwise you may not have survived.'

Saira said nothing. For a time, she lay absolutely still, eyes closed, utterly exhausted, trying to get her bearings and then she sat up, drawing up her knees and clasping her arms around them, while resting her chin against her chest. Out of the corner of her eyes, she looked at Karim Khan, taking in his broad chest and heavily muscled shoulders. This was the first time she had been alone with a man other than the male members of her immediate family, and her head was full of the stories she heard in the harem of what men did to women.

'Thank you for saving my life,' the words escaped her lips for she dared not look directly at him.

Karim Khan said nothing. Instead, he gently turned her face towards his and lowered his lips onto hers. For a fraction of a second, her mouth tightened for she had never been kissed by a man before, but then passion overbore her. Her lips parted and Karim Khan thrust his tongue deep into her mouth as he watched this lovely girl under him being transported into an ever-rising spiral of ecstasy and he bore down upon her.

As dawn broke, Karim Khan saw a rescue party in a boat heading out towards them.

Four days later as dusk was falling, Dara and his party finally stood before the gates of Lahore. Its governor, Nawab Mehboob Khan, tall and courtly, who was bound by his loyalty to the Emperor, rode out the short distance, along with his principal officers, to welcome the party. They dismounted and bowed in salutation, which Dara graciously acknowledged. After remounting, they escorted the royal party into the walled city, while the troops accompanying Dara set up camp outside its walls.

'We had asked Nawab Ifthikar Khan to send troops from Kabul to strengthen the garrison here, as we understand that our brother Aurangzeb has sent Nasri Khan in our hot

pursuit and we can expect to be attacked any day now. We
don't see those troops anywhere. Are they camping far away?'
asked Dara, leaning over the neck of his horse and addressing
Mehboob Khan, who was riding by his side.

A puzzled look crossed Mehboob Khan's face, 'To our
knowledge, Khan sahib has not despatched any troops,
Your Highness. Otherwise, he would have informed us. In any
case, no troops from Kabul are anywhere in the vicinity.'

'What?' panic seized Dara. He made an effort to control
himself. He knew that the forces he had brought with him,
in addition to those in Lahore, would be wholly inadequate
to repel Nasri Khan, let alone Aurangzeb, who was following
them. 'We had specifically directed Ifthikar Khan sahib to send
a contingent of troops along with heavy guns to strengthen the
garrison here. Did our message not reach him? Was he waylaid?
Surely, the messenger would have passed through Lahore on his
way to Kabul,' asked Dara, trying to put on a show of authority.

'I shall make inquiries,' replied Mehboob diplomatically,
looking at Dara with a certain amount of pity in his eyes,
speculating that Ifthikar must have been given prior warning
by Aurangzeb against extending any help to Dara. In fact,
such a warning had been received by Mehboob Khan, too, but
he had chosen to ignore it. He had plighted his troth to the
Emperor and he would not betray it, come what may. After all,
at eighty years of age, his honour to him was infinitely more
precious to him than his life. 'However, Raja Swarup Singh
is camping with his troops numbering around five thousand
not very far from here. His territory, as Your Highness knows,
lies in the hill country somewhat north of Lahore,' he added.
'Incidentally, Your Highness, we are informed that Nasri Khan
has been recalled and is being replaced by Bahadur Khan, as

Prince Aurangzeb has found Nasri Khan too slow in executing his orders. It is learnt that Bahadur Khan sahib, with his entourage, will be reaching the opposite bank within the next three days and has meanwhile ordered that preparations be made to cross the river, for which purpose, all the boats, carts and elephants up to twenty kos on either side of him, have been commandeered to get his guns and troops across. In fact, he has brought some boats along with him, strapped to the backs of elephants.'

At the mention of Swarup Singh's name, Dara pricked up his ears. By now, he was deeply worried whether the forces at his command would be able to repel Bahadur Khan, who was known to be one of Aurangzeb's most aggressive generals. Each additional trooper would count and, the Rajput warriors under Raja Swarup Singh appeared to be a godsend, but would he be willing to support Dara? Should Dara make the first move? If so, how? Whatever his present plight, he was the heir to the throne of Hindustan and he did not want to be seen as a supplicant, and that too before an unbeliever. Dara kept turning over the matter furiously in his mind and scarcely heard the plaudits of the welcoming crowds that had gathered in the streets of the walled city of Lahore as the party headed towards its north-western corner, through the Masjidi gate to where the heir apparent's palace was located. Crossing the thick stone walls that surrounded it and passing under a vaulted gateway within which sat drummers, trumpeters and other musicians who were playing a welcoming melody in the raga Yaman, they entered a large forecourt surrounded on all sides by a row of rooms in which resided members of the household staff. All of them stood by respectfully as the cavalcade crossed the forecourt and approached a narrower gateway leading into a smaller courtyard which gave access to the private residential apartments of the prince and was barred to all except him, the women, children and the eunuchs. At this point, Mehboob Khan and the officers with him withdrew.

Nadira, Jahanzeb and the ladies-in-waiting heaved a sigh of relief when at last they alighted in the inner courtyard of the palace to be in surroundings to which they were accustomed. Swiftly, they crossed the series of fountains, pools and canals set amidst gardens, which now with the first rains had miraculously turned a lush green, and sped up the stairs that led to their private apartments to slough off the tiredness and dust of the journey. After a much-needed bath in the ornately carved hammam, they had a light repast, and then gratefully sank into a dreamless sleep.

Meanwhile, Dara, after freshening up, was still pondering over how to tackle the raja when an aide entered, 'Raja Swarup Singh seeks audience to pay his respects, Your Highness,' said the aide.

Excellent, thought Dara to himself, heaving a sigh of relief. He now was spared from making the first move. 'We shall be happy to receive him in the Naulakha pavilion after this watch. Inform the other court officials too,' replied Dara.

For the raja, an audience with Dara was equally necessary as an immediate infusion of cash was his primary concern. His principality lay near the foothills of the Himalayas and he was returning after leading a punitive expedition to Ghazni to chastise certain refractory Afghan chieftains, but his treasure train had been looted by tribesmen while crossing the Khyber Pass, and he was left without money to pay his five thousand troops, who were getting increasingly restive with each passing day. He had heard of the wealth Dara had brought with him from the Agra treasury and pledging allegiance to the Emperor's eldest son for a price seemed the easiest way of solving his financial difficulties. True, too close an identification with Dara's cause ran the risk of incurring Aurangzeb's wrath, but that risk was relatively distant while mutiny by his troops was imminent if their demands were not satisfied. Moreover, in the next turn of fortune's wheel, was it not possible that Dara might yet set the Emperor free and in God's good time, ascend the throne? In any case, for Swarup Singh, the risk seemed worth taking.

Thus, well after the lamp lighters had gone about their business and the soft lights glittered a millionfold in the mirrors that studded the pillars and roof of the Naulakha pavilion, Raja Swarup Singh walked in with his captains to a flourish of trumpets, crossed the floor strewn with priceless carpets and bowed before Dara, who was seated on a raised divan at one end of the pavilion. The raja was a slim young man with a thin moustache and bulbous eyes and was dressed in the customary sherwani and chooridar-pajamas with a pearl-studded sarpech fastened onto his turban and a jewelled sword hanging from his waist. Dara rose slightly from his seat and with a smile gestured towards a place on the divan which was empty by his side. The sight of the putative heir to the throne of Hindustan rising in his seat to welcome his guest and seating him by his side was not lost on all those present as Raja Swarup Singh's captains took their seats opposite Dara's own officers.

'Welcome Raja sahib,' said Dara with a show of geniality. 'We have heard how effectively you dealt with these bandits around Ghazni, who had been terrorizing the area and had made the lives of traders, wayfarers and imperial officers so very difficult.'

'When the Emperor's hand is above one's head, everything is possible,' replied the raja graciously.

Both sides knew that some time would elapse in the mutual exchange of such flowery compliments before they arrived at the matter at hand.

'Indeed, well said. And would you do your bit to ensure that the Emperor's hand is restored once again over the whole of Hindustan so that all her children may dwell in peace, security and communal harmony, and each community is allowed to practise its religion without let or hindrance?' said Dara at length.

The hint at Dara's latitudinarian views in matters of religion as opposed to Aurangzeb's narrow-minded outlook, which was known throughout the empire, was too obvious to be missed, but Swarup Singh's immediate concern was cash.

'Much blood and treasure has to be expended before these admirable conditions can be realized,' the raja parried.

'No doubt. No doubt. Perhaps in confidence, with one or two of our aides, we could discuss how these conditions could be brought about,' said Dara, looking around and nodding at his officers.

At this, they took the hint and withdrew followed by the Rajput chieftain's own captains, and only Dara, Dawood Khan, Swarup Singh and his trusted aide Bhoor Singh were left in the pavilion.

'What recompense would you seek to ally your forces with ours to restore the Emperor to the throne of Hindustan?' asked Dara, coming straight to the point.

The time for circumlocution was over. With the enemy's legions rapidly advancing towards the opposite bank of the Sutlej and barely a week's march away from Lahore, some agreement with Swarup Singh that night itself was essential.

'Fifty thousand gold mohurs, Your Highness.'

'Impossible,' Dara cried. 'Your troops, we understand, do not exceed five thousand in number and are of indifferent quality, and you are asking for ten gold mohurs per head!'

'We learn that you lost most of your baggage at the Khyber Pass when your troops fled at the sight of the Afghans,' Dawood Khan added rubbing in the slight.

'Those who ran away were only the cart men, baggage carriers and labourers,' replied Swarup Singh hotly. 'My troops fought like all true Rajputs should.'

'Then what explains the loss of your treasure train?' sneered Dawood Khan.

'Come, Raja sahib. Princes don't haggle like banias in the market. Both of us have faith in our aides here. Let them work out a solution that is fair and just, to which we can give our approval,' said Dara.

A much-relieved Swarup Singh hastily assented.

Later that night, Dawood Khan reported to Dara that agreement had been reached. Swarup Singh was to receive fifteen thousand gold mohurs immediately and twenty thousand more when Shah Jahan was released from his confinement and reinstalled on the throne. Dara accorded his assent. An agreement was swiftly drawn up and fifteen sacks containing a thousand gold mohurs each were deposited in Swarup Singh's camp on the security of a hundred of Swarup Singh's troops placing themselves in Dara's custody.

Next morning, Dara summoned an aide. 'We wish to confer with cavalry commanders Sultan Mahmood and Sikander Beg, infantry commanders Multafat Khan and Naseem Haider, Master General of Ordnance Qizl Baksh Khan, Paymaster

General Askar Mohammed and Mansabdar Dawood Khan. Inform them to be present here by the next watch. Request Raja Swarup Singh also to be present. They should bring with them details of the muster roll strengths of the troops under their command, horses, guns, big and small, field pieces, gunpowder, shot and ball and all other relevant information relating to their commands.'

When the officers had assembled, Dara began without preliminaries, 'As you are aware, Agra has fallen to Prince Aurangzeb and the Emperor has been made a prisoner. Aurangzeb's general Nawab Bahadur Khan is now marching on Lahore with a large army and has reached the Sutlej. He is preparing to cross the river and his flying columns will be barely a week's march from here. Behind him is Prince Aurangzeb himself, who, in the meantime, has arrested our brother Prince Murad on the charge of murdering the diwan Ali Naqvi. It is our bounden duty to rescue the Emperor and restore him to the throne and ensure that Prince Aurangzeb receives his just deserts. Although we have suffered certain reverses at Samugarh, that is by no means the end of the story. We propose that once again, an imperial army take the field and remove this foul usurper. He is our brother and yet, words cannot describe the depths of his treason. Time is short and each day that passes helps him consolidate his hold. We seek your opinion as to what course of action we should adopt. Let your opinion be free and frank, for anything else would suit us ill at this critical juncture. We shall begin with the youngest among you, Sahebzada Naseem Haider.'

Dara followed the well-tested practice of getting the junior-most to speak up first, which would allow those senior to him to offer a contrary view without loss of face.

The young commander, brash, impetuous and eager to make an impression, cleared his throat, 'Your Highness, the foot soldiers at my command are ready to match swords with the rebel forces at any place of your choosing,' he said.

'How many men have you under your command?' Dara asked.

'Er…around three thousand,' Haider replied.

'And how many thousands do you think Bahadur Khan will bring into the field?' asked Dara, a faint sneer on his face.

'One hears that the rebels commanded over thirty thousand foot soldiers alone at Samugarh,' Multafat Khan, a senior commander, interjected. 'That excludes the cavalry and auxiliaries. Since then, several other contingents of troops from the imperial army would have defected to their ranks. Even after excluding the losses the rebels sustained at Samugarh, their effective fighting strength will not be less than what they had when they commenced their march northwards.'

'Exactly. Your three thousand will be swept away in a trice. Even if Bahadur Khan decides to leave the bulk of his army behind and crosses the river with his flying columns, your forces are unlikely to make any headway against them. Think well before you give counsel, young man,' said Dara cuttingly, looking at the youthful commander.

Chastened and crestfallen at this open snub, Naseem Haider shrank into his shell.

'Permit me, Your Highness,' began the tall, lean Askar Mohammed, the senior-most of the commanders present, who looked down over his shoulder with a supercilious eye at Naseem Haider, as if he were some strange insect and then turned to face Dara. 'In fact, knowing the reason for which we have been summoned, some of us had discussed the situation amongst ourselves before we assembled here and as desired, we will place before Your Highness the exact position regarding men and material, but the total number of troops that we could put in the field against Bahadur Khan would not exceed fifteen thousand including Naseem Haider sahib's three thousand, the troops brought by Dawood Khan sahib and the four or five thousand furnished by the local mansabdars in the parganas through which Your Highness has passed, but they will be of doubtful quality. We have only twenty-five heavy guns to repel a siege and a few more are under repairs. The lighter pieces are also in short supply, as are muskets and cavalry horses. In short, Your Highness, it is our considered opinion that Lahore and its environs is no place to face the rebels and we need to consider other options.'

'What are those?'

'This humble creature would respectfully suggest that we proceed towards Kabul and make our stand somewhere in its vicinity. The crags and passes there will act as obstacles in our favour and it will be extremely difficult for the enemy to get his heavy guns across the Khyber Pass, and the terrain will offer us some protection against being outflanked.'

'What do you have to say to that?' asked Dara, turning to Sultan Mahmood.

'There is much merit in Khan sahib's suggestion,' Mahmood replied. 'On the route to Kabul, we will be able to enlist the local mansabdars of the parganas to the imperial cause, which will add to our strength and I gather that Raja Braj Kishore Singh is camping at Sargodha with his troops, which lies on the way.'

He is the nephew of Maharaja Jaswant Singh Rathore of Marwar, who lost us the battle of Dharmat, isn't he?' interjected Dara.

'Yes, he is, Your Highness, but all aver that Maharaja sahib fought with conspicuous gallantry.'

'Well, if we can persuade Braj Kishore Singh to throw in his lot with us, we can only hope that his men put up a better performance than his uncle did at Dharmat,' said Dara drily. 'However, do continue.'

'As I was saying, Your Highness, I have just returned from a tour of inspection to Kabul and I was informed by the governor there that he had a cavalry strength of ten thousand; foot soldiers in the region of over forty thousand and sufficient numbers of cannon as well as swivel pieces and other war materiel. That should be sufficient to deter any aggressor. Of course, he was complaining of shortage of muskets, gunpowder and ball, but that can be replenished.'

'Yes, that is a possibility, but we had instructed its governor Ifthikar Khan to send reinforcements here, and he has disobeyed our instructions. We fear that our brother has threatened him with dire consequences if he opened the gates of the fort to us.'

'Ifthikar Khan is a timid man, Your Highness, and it is extremely unlikely that he would not open the gates of the fort if Your Highness appeared there in person.'

'Even if he did, we run the risk of being trapped inside.'

'The other alternative is to proceed to Multan, Your Highness,' suggested Askar Mohammed. 'The garrison there is well-equipped and can withstand a long siege.'

Dawood Khan cast an appraising eye on the commanders assembled around Dara. Most of the experienced generals had accompanied the Emperor when the court had moved to Agra and had fought and died or had been captured in the battle at Samugarh. Those that had been left behind in Lahore and were now clustered around Dara had little or no battle experience and would willingly agree to whatever Dara said. Were these the generals with whom Dara was going in to cross swords with a resolute commander like Aurangzeb? Wisely, Dawood Khan decided to say nothing. He did not have too high an opinion of Dara's military abilities either, but he had pledged his loyalties to the heir apparent and would not swerve from it.

Till late that evening, well after the hour when the sun had set and the people of Lahore were at last beginning to get some respite from the humid heat, Dara and his generals were deep in discussions on where to make the stand against Aurangzeb, but Dara was unable to make up his mind.

'You have given us valuable suggestions and we shall let you know our decision tomorrow at the second watch,' he said drawing the meeting to a close.

As soon as the conference was over, Sikander Beg rushed to his apartment. Grabbing a sheaf of paper, a quill and a pot of ink, he sped up the steep staircase that led to the roof. There, nestling in the pigeon cote was Rustam, his favourite pigeon, with its broad chest, distinctive beak, round head, thick nape and heavy cere. Sikander, who had been won over by Aurangzeb, with the promise of being made naib subedar of Awadh if he supplied regular information to his master about the happenings in Lahore, had developed an efficient homing pigeon service for carrying messages. While these pigeons normally travelled only homewards, Sikander had spent long hours overseeing the training of Rustam to travel back and forth by keeping his food at one end of the journey and his home at the other. Only a few days earlier, Rustam's trainer had pronounced him capable of carrying messages both ways and now the time had come to put the training to the test and see whether Rustam would carry Sikander's message to

Bahadur Khan, who was camping with his army across the Sutlej, ninety kos away and return home safely.

Tearing a small piece of paper from the sheaf that he had brought with him, by the light of a half-moon, Sikander scribbled the message that Dara was unlikely to make a stand at Lahore but was still undecided whether to proceed to Kabul or to flee to Multan, but a decision could be expected in a day or two.

Rolling the piece of paper tightly and then taping it to the left leg of the pigeon, he muttered a word of prayer and then looking right and left to see that no one was watching, he held the bird with both hands aloft high in the air and then threw it upwards. For a few seconds, he watched it as it fluttered to regain its balance and then gradually began to gain height and started winging its way south-eastwards.

Sikander knew that the pigeon, which could fly at an average speed of thirty kos an hour, would reach Bahadur Khan's camp well before midnight and give him invaluable lead time to decide his future course of operations.

Bahadur Khan was toying with a young virgin, when there was a discreet cough outside the flap of his tent. He put the goblet containing the wine which he was trying to coax the girl to sip on the low table near the divan on which both were reclining, and as he rose to proceed to the entrance of the tent, the girl hastily drew a coverlet upon herself to cover her nakedness.

'What is it?' Bahadur Khan asked gruffly, angered at being disturbed at his pleasures.

'A pigeon has landed in the cote nearby, All Highest. It carries a written message taped to its leg. I have brought the bird with me. As it might be important, I thought it fit to bring it to the notice of Your Highness straight away,' said the man standing outside.

Bahadur Khan turned to see that the girl had drawn a cover around herself and then parted the tent flap. There, by the light of a flaming torch which he held high in his hand, stood Yusuf, his devoted eunuch, holding in his other hand the pigeon. Bahadur Khan removed the tape from the pigeon's leg and glanced at the paper containing the message. As he did so, a smile broke his lips.

The time had come to winkle out Dara from Lahore.

Four

Meanwhile, throughout that hot, still night, Dara lay awake in his bed, his brain all awhirl mulling over the advice given to him by his generals. He watched with unseeing eyes the tassels of the giant punkah that hung from the ornate ceiling swaying from side to side, and stirring the thick air as it was pulled and released rhythmically by a slave girl by means of a stout silk rope which passed through a hole in the apartment wall into the hands of the girl who sat on the other side of it. For a brief while, the punkah came to a stop, as the girl had probably nodded off to sleep and Dara was about to get up and box her ears, when she suddenly woke up and began plying the punkah with renewed vigour upon which Dara fell back. *Let her be*, he told himself. There were far more important matters to think about. What course of action should he adopt? Prevent Bahadur Khan from any attempt to cross the swollen Sutlej a week's march away to the south by dragging what few artillery pieces he had to the riverbank and then training his guns at the likely points of crossing? Bring him to battle at an appropriate site between the riverbank and Lahore? Almost at once, he dismissed the idea of trying to repel Bahadur Khan along the banks of the Sutlej or indeed of drawing him into battle anywhere between that river and the gates of Lahore. His artillery pieces were too few, and with reinforcements from

Kabul nowhere in sight, the forces at his disposal were too meagre to even think of trying conclusions with Bahadur Khan's formidable army. They would be blown away like chaff before the wind. The only alternative then was flight, yet again, but in which direction: towards Kabul or Multan?

Was he to flee all his life, he wondered gloomily, hunted and harried like some antelope being chased and finally run to earth by a pack of ravening wolves? Would he ever be able to rescue the Emperor from his confinement if he perpetually remained on the run? And what would be the toll on his family? He glanced at Nadira slumbering peacefully by his side, she who had been brought up in the most luxurious surroundings, and had never known a single day's discomfort in her life. Already he could see that the strains of the flight since the departure from Agra were beginning to tell on her face, as callipers were forming on either side of her mouth and her once-smooth forehead was now becoming furrowed. After assuring her that they would have to flee no longer, how could he now tell her that their respite was only temporary and they would have to be on the move once more. And his sons Sulaiman and Siphir? What legacy was he going to leave to them? He remembered the night before he left Agra for Dholpur to give battle to Aurangzeb and Murad and prevent them from crossing the Chambal River; Nadira had confidently predicted victory and had prophesied that their lineage would rule the empire for as many years as there were stars in the sky. Little chance of that happening now with Sulaiman, a supplicant in the court of an unbeliever and Siphir, like himself, on the run. What dreams he and Nadira had woven about Jahanzeb marrying the scion of one of the greatest nobles of the empire in a ceremony that would be remembered down the ages as the most splendid ever held. All that was being fast reduced to ashes and dust. What was he to do? How long was he to carry these burdens? Not daring to look at her, at length he closed his eyes, trying to push aside his doubts and hesitations.

Dawn broke, and grey lowering clouds hung over Lahore city, but when despite the passage of two watches, no word had been received of the future course of action, Dawood Khan sought audience with Dara.

A burly guard and Dara's trusted eunuch Maqbool stood at the entrance to his private apartments. 'His Highness is unwell and not in a condition to receive anyone,' said Maqbool .

'It is a matter of utmost importance. Please covey that to His Highness.'

Maqbool realized that Dawood Khan would not have pressed for an audience unless the matter was really serious.

'Please wait here. I shall see what I can do,' he replied as he went inside.

A little while later, he returned. 'His Highness will receive Your Excellency, but please make it brief.'

Dawood Khan went inside and found the prince lying on a divan in his apartment, groaning in pain, as stomach cramps which gripped him at moments of indecision like these were once again resurfacing. Dara's hakeem was hovering around at the head of the divan. He had applied leeches to the prince's forearm and had assured Dara that relief would be apparent within two watches. One or two of the slugs lay twitching spasmodically in a small basin that stood nearby, as they had dropped off, gorged with blood, while another still clung to Dara's forearm. Nadira and Jahanzeb, who were ministering to Dara with cold compresses, had withdrawn behind the thick draperies at Dawood Khan's approach.

'I regret to disturb, Your Highness, but intelligence has been received that Nawab Bahadur Khan is preparing to cross the Sutlej with the bulk of his artillery tomorrow. His cavalry regiments and most of his foot soldiers completed the crossing yesterday and some of the lighter pieces along with many of the elephants and camels will be fording the river today. It is learnt that many troops and impedimenta were swept away in the fast-flowing current, but despite that, Nawab sahib decided to cross the river, as he had received a message from Prince Aurangzeb that he must effect the crossing and seize Your Highness forthwith failing which, he would suffer the same fate as his predecessor. Once the crossing is completed, it will be only a matter of time before the enemy is outside the gates of Lahore, so a decision will have to be taken swiftly, perhaps today itself.'

'Yes, yes. You shall have your decision by this evening,' replied Dara a little testily as he grimaced in pain, clutching the side of his stomach. 'These wretched cramps. They had to occur just at this hour,' he rasped through his teeth.

At once, doubts assailed the faithful courtier's mind. Dara had kept his ailment well-concealed from all except his immediate family. Could Dara have been poisoned?

'When did these attacks commence?' he asked the hakeem.

Hakeem Moinuddin Mirza was a cadaverous-looking individual with a thin scraggly beard and rheumy eyes. 'Your Excellency, I was summoned two watches ago and was told that the pains had commenced a little before that,' he quavered.

'Could it be anything His Highness ate which caused these pains?' asked Dawood Khan, his single eye boring through the hapless hakeem. 'Have the food stuffs which His Highness ate last night been preserved?'

'I am not aware of that, Your Excellency,' said Mirza. 'As I mentioned, I was only summoned two watches ago and after examining His Highness, I had sent my assistant, who was with me to fetch the medicines and the leeches so that His Highness could be bled.'

'You miserable fool,' roared Dawood Khan. 'Don't you know that His Highness's life is under constant danger and this could be a case of poisoning?'

'Quick,' he said, turning to Maqbool . 'Have the dishes and food that His Highness ate last night collected and brought here. Were those dishes not tasted by the official taster and sealed before they were laid before His Highness? If not, we shall have it tasted by him here and now. Have him brought here immediately. Incidentally, did anyone else eat from these dishes? Begum sahiba or the children?'

'No, Your Excellency, His Highness ate alone. Begum sahiba and the children said that they were not hungry, perhaps because of the heat. They only drank some sherbet.'

'Meanwhile, have all the kitchen staff and those who brought the food up to the apartments here arrested.'

A short while later, the dishes, all made of gold, which contained the food Dara had eaten were brought and laid in a row on the carpet covered with cloth, along with the head cook and the food taster.

'Did you taste the food before it was laid before His Highness?' Dawood Khan roared, fixing the taster with his single eye.

'Yes, Your Excellency', the man quavered. 'I tasted each one of the dishes and affixed my seal upon the cover before it was laid before His Highness. I have never failed in my duty before.'

'We shall see,' replied Dawood Khan grimly. 'By Allah if you have been remiss in your task, you shall not live to see the sunrise tomorrow.' Striding out of the apartment, he beckoned a guardsman who was standing outside. 'Go at once to the dungeons and fetch one of the condemned prisoners who is to be beheaded in a day or two. Tell him that His Highness, through his mercy, has decided to grant him a reprieve.'

'Anyone, Your Excellency?' the guardsman was perplexed, his brow creased in doubt.

'You fool. Don't you understand the simplest order? I said anyone. Get hold of the first man you come across who has been sentenced to death.'

'Yes, Your Excellency,' the man stammered.

Signalling to two other guards to follow him, the man raced down the flight of stairs that led to the dungeons where the prisoners who had been convicted and sentenced to death awaited their fate.

A short while later, a burly-looking prisoner was brought before Dawood Khan, who was waiting impatiently in a balcony overlooking the apartment. He was dressed in a filthy dhoti with matted hair, a beard shot through with grey, and bloodshot eyes, which darted hither and thither, expecting some trick to be played on him. Chains clanked around his ankle as he was brought forward, hands manacled behind his back.

'Come here,' said Dawood Khan soothingly as the two guards who held either arm propelled him forward. 'You have nothing to fear. His Royal Highness, in his infinite mercy, has decided to grant you a reprieve. What is more, you will be allowed to leave this palace after you have had a full meal.'

Dawood Khan signalled to a guardsman, who went inside and then reappeared with some of the dishes from which Dara had eaten the previous evening. The man's eyes widened as he saw the dishes laid before him. He had never seen so much food in his life and could not believe his good fortune.

'Here. You sit down,' said Dawood Khan, pointing towards the floor. 'Be sure you eat from every dish for these have been prepared from the royal kitchens especially for His Highness, and you will never have such a repast in your life.'

For a trice, the man hesitated. Was this some trick that was being played upon him? His eyes darted here and there, but then hunger overbore any doubts. What had he to lose? In any case, he knew that he was to be beheaded the next day and now he had been favoured with this reprieve. Perhaps the gods had been kind to him after all.

Squatting on a little mat in front of the dishes, he fell upon the food, with both hands, tasting one dish and then the other, gobbling the viands in great mouthfuls as if the next moment it would be snatched away from him. Biryani, roast fowl, venison curry, all disappeared in a trice as Dawood Khan stood over the man, watching him closely to see if there were any signs of discomfort.

When the last of the food had been consumed, a flagon of wine was brought from which Dara had drunk the previous evening. It was poured into a goblet and handed over to the man, who gulped it down greedily. When he had drunk two cupfuls of the wine and signalled that he could consume no more, and tried to rise, Dawood Khan pressed him down.

'Take some rest here. It will take some time before the kotwal authorizes your release.'

The poor man nodded. He did not know what was in store for him, but after the magnificent repast that had been laid before him, it could not be all bad. He curled up on the mat that he was sitting upon, let out a great yawn and closed his eyes.

'Keep a watch on him,' said Dawood Khan to one of the guardsmen. 'I shall be back after two watches. Meanwhile, at the least sign of discomfort or illness that he displays, let me know. Is that clear?'

The guardsman nodded his assent.

Two watches later, Dawood Khan returned. The convict was still asleep. Dawood Khan prodded him with his foot. The man opened his eyes, suddenly realized where he was and tried to stand up, but the shackles around his ankles prevented him from doing so. He looked up into Dawood Khan's single eye.

'How do you feel?' Dawood Khan asked.

'Fine, Your Excellency. Can I be released now?'

'Wait a while.'

Dawood Khan went into the inner apartments where Dara was still resting. One look at the prince reassured the courtier. Dara was sitting up and the contorted look on his face had disappeared.

'How is he?' asked Dawood Khan, looking at the hakeem.

'Much better, Your Excellency,' the hakeem replied, a faint grin creasing his gaunt face. 'I was sure that my prescription would work and indeed it has. The leeches, too, have done their duty.'

Dawood Khan glanced at the tray that stood close to where Dara reclined. Some of the leeches, purple in colour and gorged with blood had dropped off into the tray and like fat slugs twitched torpidly, while others still clung onto Dara's fingers and forearm.

'Allah be praised,' said Dawood Khan. 'I feared that His Highness may have been poisoned.' Then turning to Dara, he said. 'Time is short, Your Highness. One way or the other, a decision cannot wait much longer.'

'I am aware of that, Khan sahib. But the decision you are calling upon me to take is so grave in its import that any false step would be disastrous. All the implications have to be thought through carefully. Incidentally in the conference which we had with the generals, I noticed that you did not voice your opinion. You know how much we value your advice. What do you suggest we do?'

'I suggest we move to Multan, Your Highness and then make for Gujarat, whose governor is faithful to the Emperor and will provide the necessary reinforcements to make a bid to rescue the Emperor.'

'But Gujarat is over six hundred kos from here,' exclaimed Dara. 'We ourselves were in favour of moving to Kabul. We could seek the help of the Abbasids to mount an attack on Delhi and Agra.'

'Yes, Gujarat is quite some distance away, but I am not too sure whether any help will be forthcoming from the Abbasids. Not after they wrested Kandahar from us. In any case, what have we to offer them?' he replied, looking with a measure of exasperation at Dara. *Why was the man so incapable of taking a swift decision. All the time wavering, vacillating, undecided.* 'Moreover, God forbid we involve the Persians in our quarrels over the succession. The costs we may have to pay may be too heavy for us to bear. For the present, we only need to move to Multan, which is better defended than here. That will give Your Highness more options to decide your future course of action.'

'Well, you will have your decision soon enough,' said Dara.

'Let it be soon, Your Highness,' said Dawood Khan as he bowed and withdrew. On the way out, he ordered the prisoner to be set free, knowing that Dara would not oppose his decision.

Five

'Shall we move?' Fareed asked.

Aslam nodded.

While Dara still lay in the throes of indecision, Fareed and Aslam, with their arms around each other's necks, as if they both had had too much to drink, staggered through the narrow alleys of Lahore late that moonless night towards the block house in the south-west corner of the fort where the munitions and gunpowder were stored. Both were powerfully built individuals in Sikander Beg's pay and upon receiving a signal from Bahadur Khan, Beg had tasked them with blowing up the munitions depot that night which would render Dara defenceless and force him to flee from Lahore. Both of them were dressed in the dark-blue tunics and red turbans worn by the sentries deputed to guard the block house, and beneath Fareed's tunic, he carried a short fuse along with the flint with which to light it. They had carefully reconnoitered the area as to the best way of reaching the munitions depot and after considerable deliberation had decided that they would pose as two drunkards going home after a night's heavy drinking.

'Who goes there?' the sentry at the end of an alley asked, which opened out into a broad courtyard in the centre of which stood the vaulted, square block house in which were stored the cannonballs and gunpowder. No unauthorized person was allowed to cross the alley into the courtyard, and the block house itself was patrolled by a detachment of guards who circumambulated round the building, while sentries stood at each of the four doors, one in each wall that led into the building. High in each wall were two windows, covered with sloping eaves and protected by stout iron grills.

'Hheee ashks whoo we are,' said Fareed, looking at Aslam as they approached the sentry and peered into his face when they were barely a handspan away from him. Fareed broke out into a drunken cackle, 'Who are we? Why don't you tell him?'

'We are friends,' replied Aslam, lurching drunkenly towards the sentry till Fareed held him back. 'Friendship is the greatest boon in these uncertain times. How many friends do you have?'

The sentry stepped back, nauseated by the reeking smell that emanated from these two men.

'Be off with you,' he said curtly. 'And beware, if either of you come anywhere here again, I shall personally see that you are both locked up for good.'

Just then, Aslam pretended to stumble. The guard bent forward to prevent the man from falling on his feet, but before he could straighten up, Fareed hit him on the back of his head with a short and heavy steel club that he had brought with him. The man collapsed without a sound. They trussed him up swiftly and taped his mouth in case he cried out, and then dragged him into a small ill-frequented cul-de-sac that led off from the alley. Cautiously, they came out of the cul-de-sac and peered out of the alley at the block house, waiting till the detachment of the guard had gone past them and rounded the corner of the block house. They knew that they had very little time before the guards came around again and within that time, they had to neutralize one of the sentries who stood at the door to gain access into the block house and then set and light the fuse.

Immediately, the guards had crossed the sentry directly opposite them and rounded the corner. They sped across the intervening space and before the sentry who was sitting cross-legged nodding in sleep could raise an alarm, Fareed raised the club high in both hands and brought it down with all his might hard on the man's head, shattering his skull. Aslam searched his pockets and found a bunch of keys, the largest one of which seemed to fit the massive lock of the door that led into the block house. Using that key, Fareed swiftly opened the door and dragged the fallen sentry in, trying best as he could to avoid the blood that was trickling from the man's head onto the beaten earth.

'Quick,' Aslam muttered as he took the sentry's position at the door. 'The guards could come around any moment now.'

Fareed nodded. Inside the block house, he stuck one end of the fuse into the nearest sack of gunpowder among the sacks that covered the entire length of floor right up to the wall and then lit the other end, watching it till it caught fire. He then opened the door a crack. He could hear the captain of the guards talking to the sentry, who was at right angles to them. Closing the door softly behind them, Fareed and Aslam sped back into the alley from which they had emerged.

A series of huge explosions rocked the block house as sack after sack caught fire. Gigantic tongues of flame leaped out and could be seen licking the grills of the windows. The door through which Fareed and Aslam had entered, stood blasted open, hanging crazily on its hinges.

'What has happened?' shouted the captain of the guards as he, along with his men, rushed round the corner to the open door, but the heat, the smoke and the successive explosions that shook the building drove them back.

'Quick, get some buckets of water,' he shouted to his men. 'Where is Feroze?' he asked, referring to the sentry who was on duty.

Then, holding a piece of cloth to his nose, he peered through the open doorway. By the light of the flames, he could see the lifeless body of the sentry, lying sprawled on the ground where Fareed had dragged him.

Meanwhile, the noise of the explosions had woken Dara and Nadira from their slumber, although the royal apartments were some distance away from the block house. Dara hastily arose and went to the jharokha overlooking the city. The entire sky seemed to be shot with red and lit up with the fires, while a huge pall of smoke was rising from the direction of the block house. The air was rent with one explosion after the other and he could faintly hear the cries of the people running frantically about, not knowing what catastrophe had befallen them as they sought to save their lives and belongings.

'What has happened?' Nadira asked in a perturbed voice, sitting up in the bed.

'It seems that a fire has broken out in the direction of the block house where the munitions are stored,' replied Dara grimly. 'We shall know soon enough.'

'Oh my God!' said Nadira brokenly, fearing the worst.

Dara had just clapped his hands to summon a slave girl to send for his eunuch Khwaja Maqbool, when Maqbool himself bustled in.

'Nawab Mehboob Khan and other nobles seek audience very urgently, Your Highness,' he said, gasping for breath.

Dara nodded and entered the small hall adjacent to his

bedchamber, where he met important visitors in private.

Just then, there was a flurry at the entrance of the hall and Nawab Mehboob Khan, along with Dawood Khan and some palace officials, sought admittance. Khwaja Maqbool, who was at the doorway, showed them in.

'There have been explosions in the storeroom where the gunpowder and munitions are kept, Your Highness,' said Mehboob Khan, a worried look on his face; his normally grave composure having deserted him as Dara took in his distraught appearance. 'I am just coming from there. We are assessing the damage, but it is unlikely that we will be able to save any of the munitions. It appears to be a case of sabotage. The guards and sentries have been arrested and will be made to speak under torture, but I doubt if any of them were directly involved. We suspect it is the handiwork of Bahadur Khan's men, or persons in the pay of some of our own officers acting on a signal from Khan's approaching columns who have carried out this dastardly act.'

Mehboob Khan looked at Dawood Khan, who nodded.

'In fact, Your Highness, while coming here, we were discussing among ourselves and we feel it will not be safe for you to stay here any longer. Bahadur Khan's men may well have infiltrated into the fort and your own life may be in grave danger. We strongly suggest that you move from here,' said Dawood Khan.

'Yes, Dawood Khan sahib here has been pressing us to decide whether to proceed to Kabul or Multan and we have been thinking over the matter, but we don't want to be hustled into taking a decision which we might rue later. We have just reached here, and if Bahadur Khan has plans to attack us, we are ready to resist him as best as we are able to,' said Dara indignantly. 'We have not come this far just to run again.'

'Resist him with what, Your Highness?' said Dawood Khan, with some asperity in his voice, as if trying to explain something to a stubborn child who refused to understand. 'There may be a few sacks of gunpowder lying near the gun emplacements, but the bulk of it was stored in the block house and that has been blown up. If Bahadur Khan were to attack now, we will be completely defenceless, and there is no time to replenish the stocks. Moreover, if those who set off the explosions are infiltrators, and we have strong reasons to suspect they are, others may also have entered the city. During the day, the gates are opened and it is not humanly possible to keep track of each and every person who comes in or goes out. In fact, Your Highness, it may be difficult to guarantee your safety and that of Begum sahiba inside the walls of the fort.'

'And where do you suggest we flee to?' asked Dara, a faint sneer lacing his voice.

Dawood Khan ignored the jibe. He had sworn fealty to the Emperor and he saw it as his duty to protect the person whom he saw to be the legal heir as best as he could, even at the cost of being absolutely blunt. 'I suggest Multan, Your Highness. It's over a hundred kos from here. Your Highness will be safe there from Bahadur Khan's men for the present at any rate till we can devise some other plan.'

Mehboob Khan nodded in assent.

'Ah, Multan. It is famous for its Sufi shrines including the mausoleum of Shah Gardez. We have always wanted to visit it. Let us think it over. We will have to consult Begum sahiba too. Such a grave decision cannot be taken in a hurry.'

'I beg of your good self to take a decision in the matter without any delay, Your Highness. As soon as news reaches

Bahadur Khan that the munitions have been blown up, he will lose no time in fording the river, whatever the cost to him and attacking us here, knowing that we will be at his mercy. We cannot afford to tarry. It is advisable that the party moves this night itself. Every moment is precious. Meanwhile, I shall make arrangements for the journey,' replied Dawood Khan.

Dara dismissed the nobles with a curt nod and went inside his bedchamber. 'It was Nawab sahib and Dawood Khan. They have come straight from the ammunition storehouse. They say that most of the gunpowder has been blown up and advise us to flee to Multan to avoid capture by Bahadur Khan, as we have been rendered defenceless. They advise that we move this night itself to avoid possible capture,' he said to Nadira.

'Ya Allah,' Nadira groaned in a hoarse whisper. 'Are we perpetually to be hounded from one city to the other with no rest?' Won't Bahadur Khan's men follow us to Multan?'

'That is why we have to put as much distance as possible between him and us to minimize that risk, and for the present, Multan is the safest place till we formulate further plans. Moreover, if worst comes to worst, it will give us access to the Gomal Pass into Afghanistan,' replied Dara. 'Now with the ammunition all blown up, if we remain here, we will be like rats caught in a trap.'

Nadira did not remonstrate any further. On reaching Lahore, she had gathered from gossip in the harem that Sulaiman's army had dissolved and he himself had sought refuge in a court in Garhwal, which explained Dara's evasiveness whenever she had questioned him about father and son coordinating their plans to attack Aurangzeb jointly. So, no help could be expected from that quarter. It was also common knowledge that Ifthikar Khan had sent no troops from Kabul to shore up Lahore's strength and now with the stock of ammunition blown up in the fort, she realized that what Dara was saying was indeed true. There was no alternative but to flee.

Preparations were made that night itself for their departure. Siphir and Jahanzeb were woken up and asked to get ready, essentials were packed, the carriages were brought out and the camels and horses harnessed, and well before dawn broke, Dara, Nadira and the two children, with an escort party of around five hundred horsemen under the command of Dawood Khan, left Lahore bound for Multan. Four days later, they found themselves approaching the fort with the waters of the Chenab River shimmering in the morning sunlight.

Outriders were sent out to have the gates opened to receive the party, but they soon returned conveying the refusal of the fort's governor Tufail Mohammed to do so.

Now what? wondered Dara, feeling increasingly desperate. He did not want a repetition of the events that had occurred outside the gates of Delhi.

Just then an outrider who had been deputed by Dawood Khan in one of the villages close to Lahore to keep an eye on Bahadur Khan's movements rode up.

'I have…an urgent report for Nawab Dawood Khan sahib,' he blurted between gasps as guards surrounding Dara barred his way.

Dawood Khan, who at that moment was engaged in discussions with Dara, went towards the man. 'What is it?' he asked.

'Units of Nawab Bahadur Khan's cavalry are now less than two days' march from Multan, Your Excellency,' he exclaimed as he paused to draw breath. 'They bypassed Lahore altogether and crossed the Sutlej at a point where his horsemen could ford the river and are making straight for Multan. His artillery and infantry are following behind.'

'Any idea of the strength of these columns?'

'Not less than two thousand, Your Excellency. The regular units behind them are of course far greater in number. It is rumoured that Prince Aurangzeb is dissatisfied with the tardy progress made by Nawab sahib and is himself moving with his whole army towards Multan to direct operations personally.'

Dawood Khan recounted to Dara what his outrider had told him. 'The best course of action would be to leave Multan immediately and go via Sindh to Gujarat, Your Highness.' He added, 'The governor, Tufail Mohammed, must have been warned by Prince Aurangzeb that he would open the fort gates at his own peril. We would be wasting time to get him to open it. Every moment is precious. Bahadur Khan and his men will be held off as much as possible, but with the forces at our disposal, it is unlikely that we will be able to do so for more than a few hours out here in the open plain, as he will throw into battle all that he has, knowing that Prince Aurangzeb is bringing up reinforcements.'

'But Gujarat is more than three hundred kos,' said Dara plaintively. 'How far will we keep running? We had much rather face Bahadur Khan and if necessary, Aurangzeb here, on the battlefield, and perish in the attempt, rather than keep on fleeing.'

'Face Bahadur Khan and possibly even Prince Aurangzeb with what, Your Highness?' Dawood Khan scoffed. 'We have brought around five hundred persons with us and they are of indifferent quality. We have no artillery. The troops will be wiped out within the hour. Instead, I suggest that it be made to appear that Your Highness is moving towards the Gomal Pass to enter Afghanistan. Meanwhile, you head south towards Sindh and thence to Gujarat. By the time they realize the deception, it will give us time, and if the lead is sufficient, it is unlikely that Bahadur Khan or for that matter, Prince Aurangzeb will follow your good self deep into Sindh and leave affairs in the north unattended. Prince Shuja still retains imperial ambitions and any vacuum in the north will promptly be filled by him. Moreover, think of the fate of Begum sahiba and Your Highness's children if Allah forbid, Your Highness were to… er…be captured, or worse still, fall in battle here.'

'But how do we get to Sindh? Won't we be intercepted by the very men we will be fleeing from?'

'We can proceed to Mithankot, which is two days' distance from here, Your Highness, where the Chenab, Ravi and Jhelum meet the Indus River. Several groups of pilgrims gather there and then travel by boat down the Indus River towards Thatta in Sindh to pray at the dargah of Diwan Sharfu Khan, the renowned Sufi divine, and some of them then proceed even further south to board dhows and sail along the coast towards Arabistan and Mecca sharif on haj. The main risk is only till the time we reach Mithankot, for once we reach there, we will mingle with the scores of pilgrims gathered there and we will be able to lose ourselves among them. I shall make out that I am proceeding to Thatta in fulfilment of a vow that I had taken and you, Begum sahiba and the children are my relatives who are accompanying me. We will wear the clothes of ordinary travellers, so as not to attract suspicion. All the talking will be done by me, and it can further be conveyed that you have taken a vow not to speak till you have prayed at the dargah, which will avoid your having to answer any inconvenient questions. In Mithankot, the pilgrims are composed of several different groups, coming from far-flung parts of the country, who speak many different tongues not understood by others, and each group stays pretty much to themselves. Each person lives within his group and if we take certain basic precautions, we are unlikely to be detected. Moreover, Begum sahiba and Jahanzeb will be protected with the hijab from prying eyes. From Thatta, we will have to engage reliable guides to take the party across the Raan of Kutch to Ahmedabad, but such guides are available, of course, for a hefty fee. Meanwhile, Karim Khan will lead a strong party westward, with carriages and other equipage to make out that you are heading for the Gomal Pass and thence to Afghanistan, which hopefully will divert Bahadur Khan's men in that direction.'

'Will this plan of yours work?' asked Dara, sounding dubious.

'What is the alternative, Your Highness? With Bahadur Khan's men less than two days away and the gates of Multan fort closed, no other proposition appears feasible. As I mentioned, the fear of incurring Prince Aurangzeb's wrath is so great that here, too, as in Delhi, the chances of the fort's gates being opened are negligible. Meanwhile, we will be losing precious moments in futile negotiations.'

Dara realized the correctness of Dawood's advice in view of the difficult situation they found themselves in. He went and explained it to Nadira. By now, she was past caring where her husband took her and heard Dara out without even a murmur. The plan was put into operation swiftly. To avoid attracting unnecessary attention, the party that was to proceed to Thatta was pared down to the minimum and was now to consist only of Dara, Dawood Khan, Nadira, Siphir, Jahanzeb, Maqbool and Saira. The large spacious carriages in which the ladies had travelled this far were exchanged for smaller but swifter ones, and members of the party shed their expensive-looking clothes for far humbler ones as befitting those going on a pilgrimage.

Dawood Khan summoned Karim Khan. 'Upon you rests the fate of the prince imperial and the release of the Emperor from incarceration by a foul usurper,' he said, fastening the tall captain with his single eye and explaining the purpose of the mission. 'Bahadur Khan's men must be distracted by making it look to all as if Prince Dara and his family are fleeing into Afghanistan through the Gomal Pass, which will give us enough time to reach Mithankot and sail down the Indus towards Thatta. The longer you are able to delay Bahadur Khan, the better it is for us.'

Karim Khan nodded, saluted respectfully and turned the bridle of his horse. Digging his spurs into its flanks, he signalled the troops to follow him with a sweep of his arm and then led them past the fort towards the north-west. There was no time to say his farewell to Saira.

The party now proceeded at breakneck speed towards Mithankot, overtaking several carriages, bullock carts, horsemen and pilgrims travelling on foot towards that town. The jolting of the carriage on the rutted potholed road threw Nadira and Jahanzeb off balance quite a few times and they held on for dear life at whatever support the carriage offered as it rocked and swayed its way to their destination, throwing up great clouds of dust in the process.

Two evenings later, they reached the spot where the waters of the Ravi, Chenab and Jhelum met the Indus and a little further down river were the steps around which were grouped flat-bottomed boats of different sizes with their boatmen shouting for custom amidst scores of pilgrims who were pushing and jostling each other in a scene of indescribable confusion and were busy haggling to get the cheapest rates for the boat journey.

'Come, Master,' a youngish-looking, thickset boatman cried as he ran up the steep sandy riverbank and accosted Dawood Khan, who had paid off the coachmen and was busy shepherding the party towards the boats. 'Where does My Lord and his party want to proceed to? Sukkur? Beyond that to Thatta? See my boat over there, Your Excellency? It is brand new and will take you wherever My Lord desires.' He pointed towards a boat with a high prow and gaily coloured cushions. The boat, tied to a wooden stake on the riverbank and bobbing in the waters a little away from the others, could seat around a dozen people. A rattan awning provided shade for only about half the boat.

It suited Dawood Khan perfectly. 'How much?' he asked shortly.

'Three gold mohurs for each day, Your Excellency. I shall reach you to Sukkur in ten days and another five days to Thatta.'

The rates were steep, but with Bahadur Khan hot on their heels, it was not the time to haggle.

Dawood Khan nodded. 'How soon can we leave?' he asked.

'Within this watch, Your Excellency.'

Upon Dawood Khan signifying his agreement and paying a small advance, the party loaded the few belongings they had brought along with them into the boat and then clambered in. Two other colleagues of the boatman also jumped in and with the aid of stout poles, the boat was propelled into the current of the river.

By now, night had fallen, and a thin moon hung in the

starlit sky which picked out the dark brooding mass of the river almost as broad as the sea, which seemed to stretch interminably into the distance. Nadira, Jahanzeb and Saira made themselves as comfortable as they could on the benches that lined the boat under the awning and promptly fell asleep, while Dara, Dawood Khan and Maqbool took turns at keeping an eye on the boatmen.

Throughout the night, the boatmen took turns in guiding the boat forward, singing a monotonous dirge as they hugged the bank of the river, and allowed the boat to drift with the current, now and then digging their poles into the shallow sandy loam that lined the riverbank to propel the boat forward. The morning found them opposite a small village set atop a high embankment.

'We can stretch ourselves here,' said Dawood Khan as he signalled to the boatman to moor the boat along the lip of the river, some distance away from other boats similarly moored on the riverbank.

Taking care to avoid the other pilgrims, the party got down to stretch their legs, perform their ablutions and make some purchases of condiments in the village for their onward journey. A fire was lit and the party had a modest repast. Soon, they were on their way again.

'Well, Karim Khan seems to have deflected attention from us,' remarked Dara to Dawood Khan as they got back into the boat. 'The fact that we have not been pursued all this while since we left Multan indicates that your plan has been successful and the deception has worked.'

In actual fact, it was less Karim Khan's diversionary tactics, and more the report a galloping courier had brought to Aurangzeb, who was four days' march away from Multan, that Shuja had crossed the border of Bengal and was marching upcountry towards Agra with an enormous army that made him abruptly order Bahadur Khan to call off his pursuit of Dara and join him in rushing headlong north-eastwards to face this fresh challenge to his dominion. Meanwhile, the little party sailed down the storied river Indus. As Mithankot fell away and the danger of being overwhelmed by Bahadur Khan's columns receded, Dara and his entourage began to breathe more easily. They settled themselves into a regular routine of camping for the duration of one watch each morning on the bank of the river to perform their ablutions and cook their meal for the day, while the rest of the time was spent on the boat carrying them to their destination.

Days thus passed in unceasing procession and all sense of time seemed to be lost as the flat, dun-coloured landscape scarcely ever changed. The broad river, now dotted with the boats of pilgrims, appeared to blend almost imperceptibly with its banks on either side as far as the eye could see, and its slow, sluggish current hardly made a ripple on its surface as the boats wended their way forward. Occasionally, a village could be spotted nestling drowsily along the riverbank on slightly higher ground, untouched by the passage of time, barely visible above the reeds which clogged the marshland with bright patches of green and a cluster of trees to break the monotony of the landscape, where embankments had been raised to tap the river water for irrigation. The cries of villagers could at times be heard going about the immemorial tasks of daily rural life—fishermen engaged in their daily catch, their womenfolk busy with their household chores or children gambolling in the river water, but otherwise a vast emptiness seemed to engulf all under the canopy of the sky.

The party navigated the Sukkur gorge, where the Indus narrowed between limestone hills. Here, the rush of the current gained pace, only to fan out again and allow the river to resume its slow, sluggish, meandering course as they crossed the little town of Bhakkar, and at length, found themselves in lower Sindh, sailing past the glittering dome of the newly constructed Jamia Masjid in Thatta.

Dara was feverish with excitement at having reached Thatta, for within the vast necropolis of Makhli nearby was the dargah of Hazrat Abdullah Shah Ashabi, the great Muslim divine who had travelled all the way from Baghdad nearly half a millennium earlier.

'It has been one of my ambitions to visit the dargah of Hazrat sahib,' said Dara to Dawood Khan as their boat reached the steps of the ghat that led up to the town. 'When I was a boy, my teacher, Mullah Abdul Latif Saharanpuri, used to cite the precepts of Hazrat sahib so very often on the importance of learnings and adjured me to visit his dargah if I ever happened to visit Thatta. Now, I have that good fortune though I could only wish the circumstances had been more propitious.'

The party found themselves a fairly secluded corner of a sarai where other pilgrims were lodged, and after making arrangements to ensure that Nadira and the children were provided a modicum of privacy under the watchful eye of Dawood Khan, Dara and Maqbool hastened their steps towards the mausoleum of Hazrat Abdullah Shah. Wayfarers gave them the necessary directions to the mausoleum within the necropolis, with its profusion of sandstone domes, platforms, cupolas and structures, in several different styles, and soon, they stood before the modest-looking tomb, where they paid their obeisance.

By happenstance, just then the muezzin sounded the call to prayer and Dara hastily proceeded to the mosque that stood close by. There, as he knelt down to perform the sajda, tears of ecstasy rolled down his face. He recollected the words of Hazrat Abdullah Shah on the illimitable majesty of the universe, much of which was hidden from view of mortal man, beyond which lay still deeper realities, whose depths only true believers in Allah could reach. Had not fate, however harsh, brought him to the tomb of his preceptor? As a true believer, was this not a sign of divine dispensation? Would not the path forward for him now be eased?

Away in the sarai, Nadira's mind was occupied with more mundane thoughts. For some time now, she had been racked by a cough, with streaks of blood that speckled the sputum, which did not seem to subside, despite the hakeem's ministrations. It was getting increasingly difficult to keep her condition away from her husband much longer. She knew that beyond Thatta, there lay the trackless wastes of the Sindh desert and beyond that the pitiless Rann of Kutch, which they would have to cross before the walls of the Ahmedabad Fort drew near. Would her body be able to stand up to the journey?

Six

'Bput try as we might, Panditji, we find it difficult to understand how your religion can describe the whole world as illusionary. Are we an illusion? Are all of us sitting here an illusion? The day, the night, the birds, the sky, all that we can touch and see and taste and feel, are they all illusions? Yes, we grant you the concept of the individual soul... what do you call it...yes, the atman. Doesn't it...being a part of the universal soul or Brahman, bear considerable resemblance to our own Tauheed-e-Ilahi, practised by our Sufis or mystics? Like your own babas or mendicants, we, too, have our mureeds, who seek personal salvation through mystical union with Allah, but to say that the only reality is Brahman and all else that we see around us is merely maya or illusion...' Dara left the rest of the sentence unsaid, his brow furrowed in doubt.

It was a few days after Dara and his party had reached Ahmedabad without mishap and had been offered refuge by the governor of Gujarat, Nawab Shah Nawaz Khan. Winter had set in a little early and there was a slight nip in the air as Dara sat in his apartment in the Rang Mahal overlooking the Sabarmati River as its waters flowed sluggishly by. Around him sat savants and divines of different faiths. All night long, the discussions had continued in what was Dara's lifelong ambition—to find a common meeting ground between Islam and Hinduism, and as the arguments grew more spirited, stretching far into the night, the oil lamps which had been placed at regular intervals around the group at the start, and which were being regularly replenished had now stared guttering. Some of the flunkeys and servitors in attendance tried desperately to stifle their yawns even as they stood in their positions while others found some convenient pillar or alcove in the apartment to recline against, just waiting for the discussions to conclude and the gathering to rise so that they could retire for the night.

'That is only one school of thought, My Lord. It is called the Advaita School,' said a pandit from Benares with a faint sneer. 'It was founded by Shankaracharya of Kaladi. Indeed, My Lord is correct when he observes that it is difficult to categorize the entire phenomenal world as being illusionary with objective reality. There are other schools too, one of which is called Vishishtadvaita, which was founded by Ramanujacharya, into whose teaching I was initiated by my guru, Swami Akhileshwarananda of Haridwar. It corresponds more nearly to the real world as we see it. According to it, the jivatma is a part of and is similar to Brahman, but is not identical to it. Indeed, it avoids the mistake of describing the entire phenomenal world as being illusionary and has a place for Brahman as well as for corporeal matter and the souls as distinct but mutually inseparable entities.'

The pandit was in full flow, pleased that he had gained Dara's ear, but just then an attendant entered and bowed. 'My Lord Nawab Shah Nawaz Khan seeks private audience urgently, Your Highness,' he said.

'We shall continue these discussions sometime later,' said Dara to the group and as they rose to make their exit, Dara nodded at the attendant.

Just then, Shah Nawaz Khan entered the apartment. He was Aurangzeb's father-in-law but was incensed at the treatment meted out by his son-in-law to the Emperor and had opened the gates of Ahmedabad Fort to Dara, whom he considered the rightful heir to the throne. As the savants filed past him, Shah Nawaz shook his head in disbelief, wondering if Dara had it in him to defeat his dour, single-minded brother and set the Emperor back on the throne. While the imperial fabric in Hindustan was being rent asunder by the ruthless ambitions of Aurangzeb, the putative heir to the throne was engaged in hair-splitting over abstruse religious minutiae which were of little concern except to religious scholars.

'Welcome, Khan sahib,' said Dara affably. 'To what do we owe this visit at such a late hour?'

'I bear grave tidings, Your Highness. The rumours about Aurangzeb being trounced by Shuja are all false. Perhaps they were put out by Aurangzeb himself to persuade you to make a rash move. Authentic information has just reached me confidentially that Shuja has been severely mauled by Aurangzeb at a battle near a village called Khajwa, close to Allahabad. Despite his enormous number of war elephants, Prince Shuja's forces were no match for Prince Aurangzeb's army, comprising over ninety thousand soldiers and he is now being chased eastwards by Aurangzeb's general Mir Jumla through Bihar towards Bengal and the Arakan forests.'

Dara remained silent for a while. Reports had been filtering through for some time past that Aurangzeb was moving east from Agra with a huge army to crush Shuja once and for all, and rumours had reached Ahmedabad that Aurangzeb had been worsted in battle, which had dispelled the gloom in Dara's camp. Shuja's defeat now put paid to any hopes Dara had of obtaining Shuja's assistance in attacking Aurangzeb. He realized that his hated brother would now turn upon him with all his wrath and fury. Dara paused for a moment. Was Shah Nawaz telling the truth? Was the information of Shuja's defeat correct? After all, was not Shah Nawaz Aurangzeb's father-in-law and was this some elaborate plot hatched by the two to trap him, whose contours for the moment he could not immediately discern? Should what Shah Nawaz had said not be got independently verified? That could be done later. For the moment, Dara put the doubts out of his mind. Shah Nawaz had given him shelter when he had needed it most and helped him raise an army exceeding twenty thousand. His fealty to the Emperor was without question. The information he had brought could not for the moment be doubted.

'Well, we think this makes it all the more necessary for us to move north as soon as possible before Prince Aurangzeb is able to consolidate his hold over Hindustan,' said Dara after some time. 'As you know, Zorawar Singh, a trusted aide of Maharaja Jaswant Singh Rathore of Marwar, sought audience with us yesterday and we have received assurances from the Maharaja that he would be willing to join forces with us in our advance on Delhi and Agra. With him as an ally, other Rajput chieftains are sure to follow.'

'Your Highness, I would not place much trust in these assurances. Let us not forget that Maharaja Jaswant Singh had pledged his allegiance to Prince Aurangzeb, but according to reports just received, he broke his word at the last minute, and hung back in the battle at Khajwa instead of attacking Shuja's formations. It seems that a little before the battle, he had received a secret promise from Shuja that he would look the other way if Jaswant expanded westward towards Jaisalmer which he has been coveting since long. It is another matter that despite the Maharaja's hanging back, Prince Aurangzeb was able to prevail.'

'Well, in the course of his submissions, Zorawar clearly mentioned his master's complete disinterest in expanding towards Jaisalmer. You know how touchy these Rajputs are on questions of honour. Could it be that the Maharaja hung back when the battle was progressing only because he was not allowed to lead the van in the battle, and some other Rajput chieftain was called upon to do so which the Maharaja must have taken as a mortal slight? Don't forget that some such contretemps occurred during the battle of Samugarh, too, and we were hard put to bring about a degree of amity between the Kachhwaha and the Chandela chieftains.'

'That explanation would not convince anyone, Your Highness,' replied Shah Nawaz Khan bluntly. 'How could the Maharaja even think of leading the van, especially when Prince Aurangzeb's eldest son Sultan Muhammad was present on the battlefield and would have that honour by right? Indeed, knowing Prince Aurangzeb, it seems a miracle that he even let Maharaja Jaswant Singh command a division in his army after defeating him at Dharmat last year. Does Your Highness plan to give the Maharaja a prominent role in the campaign under your supervision?' Shah Nawaz Khan persisted.

'Well, Zorawar Singh said that Jaswant wants a chance to avenge his defeat at Dharmat and we want to give him that. We will, of course, keep a close eye on him throughout the campaign. One advantage, of course, is that as head of the Rajput confederacy, he will be able to rally other princes of that warrior race to the Emperor's cause. Can you suggest any alternative course of action?'

'Go with your army to the Deccan, Your Highness,' replied Shah Nawaz Khan earnestly. 'If the rumours about Aurangzeb being defeated by Shuja were deliberately circulated on Aurangzeb's orders, it was clearly to inveigle you to march northwards as speedily as possible and grapple with him at a place of his own choosing. It is among the Deccan's crags and hills that Prince Aurangzeb built his own army before he moved north. Perhaps Your Highness could take a leaf from his book. Your Highness is sure to find ready support there. The Marathas and the other Hindu kingdoms in the Deccan had become fed up with Prince Aurangzeb's exactions during his viceroyalty and now that he is assuming regal pretensions, there is widespread belief that as soon as he fastens his grip on the empire, he will impose the jizya, which is hated by the Hindus. Both Adil Shah of Bijapur and Qutub Shah of Golconda have faced Prince Aurangzeb's whiplash and would do anything to rid themselves of his shackles. Also, you will find ready support from young Shiva, who is known as Shivaji among his Maratha people. Your Highness is sure to be welcomed in the Deccan and Aurangzeb knows that as long as that region is not firmly in his grasp, his claim to be overlord of Hindustan will be insecure. If Maharaja Jaswant Singh wants to wipe out the stain of his defeat at Dharmat, let him lead the expedition against Prince Aurangzeb, supported by any of the leading Mughal generals, but I would not advise that Your Highness try conclusions with Aurangzeb unless you have consolidated your strength in the Deccan.'

'But that is going in a direction absolutely opposite to the one we need to take if we are to release the Emperor from his confinement,' Dara countered. 'If we withdraw and proceed south, it will be apparent to the world that we are not ready to face Aurangzeb, and in effect, it will be ceding the whole territory from Afghanistan to Bengal to him, if as you say Prince Shuja is already on the run after his defeat at Khajwa. Our main anxiety is to free the Emperor, and if we proceed towards the Deccan, instead of marching north, he, too, will have given up any hope of being freed. We have to keep his hopes alive if not anything else.'

'Do not consider it ceding of any territory, Your Highness, but look upon it as consolidation of your own strength. Times arise in the affairs of princes, when it becomes necessary to effect what might seem even a withdrawal for tactical reasons, so that one may prevail with greater force at a later date. This is one of those times. Moreover, there is another reason. If Prince Aurangzeb sees the Deccan rising in your support, he is bound to lead an expedition down South and it will be far easier to defeat him with comparatively smaller numbers than it would require to defeat him on his own terrain as his lines of communication will be dangerously overstretched. Now that Shuja has been trounced, I need hardly stress, Your Highness, that Prince Aurangzeb would like nothing better than to fight a set-piece battle on the plains of Hindustan where his lines are short and numbers would prevail.'

'What you say has considerable merit, Khan sahib. Rest assured we shall give it our most careful consideration.'

'Whatever course of action you adopt, Your Highness, there is one suggestion I have to make and it needs to be implemented with the utmost speed,' said Shah Nawaz.

'What is that?'

'Before any campaign is launched, Surat should be occupied. Its killedar, Abdul Tayyib, has gone over to the rebels and is refusing to send the annual tribute to our coffers here. In fact, he is not responding to any of my letters. Lord Murad ransacked Surat and compelled the merchants there to extend a loan to finance the campaign and we should do the same, as any campaign to conquer Agra and rescue the Emperor will require funds. Moreover, Surat has a formidable artillery park and those cannon will be extremely useful in any encounter with Aurangzeb.'

'Yes, indeed. We will require considerable funds to mount the campaign and as far as we can see, Surat will provide that. And the cannon will no doubt be very useful. Whom do you suggest should be placed in command of the expedition to Surat?'

'I can think of none better than Qizl Baksh Khan. He is energetic and aggressive, and although he is a cavalry commander, he has good knowledge of artillery, which will be useful in case Surat has to be besieged.'

Qizl Baksh Khan was a short, thick-set person with bow legs, the result of too much riding. Opinion was divided whether he was a eunuch. The general view was that the operation had not been fully successful and did not interfere with his pleasures.

'Permit me to make another point, Your Highness,' continued Shah Nawaz Khan smoothly. 'The merchants and the well-to-do in Surat will not part with their wealth readily. Some…er…coercive measures might become necessary to make them more amenable to cooperate. These measures will be kept to the minimum of course, but even so, some of them will be distasteful. However, unless they are taken, the expedition is likely to return empty-handed. In due course, some complaints may reach Your Highness of the methods employed. Qizl Baksh and his officers will hope that undue attention is not paid to those complaints.'

Dara looked at Shah Nawaz Khan intently for a brief second and then looked away.

The Khan had his answer.

Surat is ninety kos due south of Ahmedabad and dragging his siege train behind him, Qizl Baksh Khan reached the outskirts of the city with his six thousand troops on the fifteenth day of leaving Ahmedabad. Meanwhile, information of the progress of the approaching force was being given regularly by his spies to the killedar of Surat, Sayyid Talib—a tough, grizzled veteran, who had switched sides and sworn allegiance to the rising star. Correctly assessing that the population inside the fort could not be protected by the numerically small garrison at his disposal, he had withdrawn the bulk of the city's defenders behind it, together with the richer merchants and their wealth, and it was mainly those who could not buy their way inside the fort or were literally penniless that were left to face Qizl Baksh Khan's exactions. There were few to defend them and for three days and nights, they were subjected to the most inhuman forms of torture to disgorge what little they had. Houses, even of the poorest, were put to the torch; women were raped in the presence of their elders; children were impaled with spears in the presence of their loved ones; old grey beards had their eyes gouged out or their noses sliced before their heads were hacked off; boiling oil or water was forced down the throats of others and even the absolutely destitute were burned alive in the hope that at least in their dying agonies, they would divulge where they had hidden some miserable copper coins. Indeed, for those left outside the fort during that period, a quick death itself seemed like an act of mercy, as their wails and shrieks rent the air, and were clearly audible to all those cowering behind the ramparts of the fort.

Having satisfied himself that nothing more was to be had
from those living outside its walls, Qizl Baksh set about appealing
to Tayyib's cupidity to secure entry into the fort. Among Qizl
Baksh's entourage was a person named Ali Kamran, who was
known to Tayyib. Qizl Baksh sent for Kamran one night.

'You sent for me, Sahib?' asked Kamran as he approached
Qizl Baksh sitting alone in his tent by the light of a single oil
lamp.

'Yes. How well do you know Sayyid Talib?'

'Very well indeed. We hail from the same pargana in Awadh
and both of us studied in the same seminary in Jaunpur. We
have also been from time to time stationed at the same or
nearby places, and our friendship has continued.'

'Can you carry a message from me to him? Under signs of
truce, of course. It might help shorten this fruitless struggle.'

'Certainly.'

'Then go tell him that further resistance is useless. He
has already seen what I have done to the people of Surat
living outside its walls, and the same fate will befall those living
within if they continue to resist. Tell him that His Majesty
Shah Jahan is still overlord of Hindustan and Lord Dara is
his anointed heir. This fruitless struggle, in which his defeat is
certain, can be ended in an instant if he delivers the fort to
us. I have the authority of Lord Dara to promise him that if
he does so, no harm will befall him or his family.'

'Early next morning under a flag of truce, Kamran rode
across the wide esplanade which provided the only landward
access to the fort. They proceeded under the shadow of the
cannon mounted on its ramparts.

Tayyib received him courteously. 'We meet under
unfortunate circumstances, my friend. What brings you under

the barrels of my guns to this fort?'

Kamran conveyed Qizl Baksh's message to Tayyib.

The warrior listened in silence to what Kamran said and then replied, 'It is only because you are an old friend of mine that I am not reacting to this proposal more violently. If it had been anyone else, I would have sent back his head at the point of a lance. I have pledged my sword to Prince Aurangzeb and I cannot go back on my word now.'

Baulked of his efforts to seize the fort through bribes and blandishments, Qizl Baksh decided to invest it from the esplanade side. Siting his cannon at regular intervals, he commenced the bombardment on the morning of the fourth day after reaching Surat. Unfortunately for him, in his haste to get to grips with the enemy, he had left some of his heavy cannon behind and the comparatively lighter pieces that were available in his siege train were easily outranged by the heavy artillery mounted on the battlements of the fort.

'We shall have to take the fort by direct assault,' he told his captains, when the siege had dragged on for some days without making much headway. 'Prepare the assault parties, with ladders, grappling irons and all the other equipment. Meanwhile, we shall concentrate our fire on the main gate of the fort which might weaken and crack to let in our storming parties.'

Within the fort, when the assault seemed imminent, Tayyib exhorted the defenders. 'Men, despite nearly ten days of sustained artillery barrages, the enemy has failed to breach our defences because of the bravery displayed by each and every one of you. Now he hopes to defeat us by a direct assault, and I have no doubt that we will give him a befitting reply this time too. We have pledged our sword to Prince Aurangzeb, under whose rule, this land of ours will truly become a Dar al-Islam and we should be prepared to lay down our lives to protect that cause and the laws of our faith. Life indeed is precious, but more precious than life is honour to our religion, and those who are unwilling to offer the supreme sacrifice will assuredly find no place in the garden of Allah.'

Fortified by these uplifting words, the defenders got ready to repel the assault. Time and again, Qizl Baksh hurled his troops against the fortress, but each time, accurate and deadly fire from the gun emplacements on the fortress walls, coupled with the musket and arrow volleys from the defenders, forced the attackers back. A few of Qizl Baksh's men did succeed in crossing the moat, reaching the fortress walls and even placing scaling ladders against it, but huge buckets of boiling oil and naphtha poured over them from top sent them plunging into the moat in agony.

Baffled by these repulses, Qizl Baksh was discussing with his commanders what further strategy to adopt, when one of them spoke up. 'Your Excellency, there is a feringhee in one of my detachments. He was telling some of my men that the only way to get close to the fort would be to dig tunnels right up to the ramparts and then mine the walls. He has one of those unpronounceable feringhee names, but because of his red hair, he is generally known as Lalbal.'

Qizl Baksh looked at his commanders and they at him. 'Bring this feringhee here at once,' he commanded.

A short while later, a tall, well-built young man was ushered into Qizl Baksh's tent. Apart from his fair complexion, which made it obvious that he was of Caucasian descent, what was striking about him was his flaming red hair, which seemed to rise practically from his eyebrows and then fell in a great mane on his shoulders. William Vandevelde was a twenty-nine-year-old Dutch soldier of fortune. As a young man of twenty, he had enlisted as a private in the armies of the Elector of Hanover and had served there for nearly five years, but finding that he was being repeatedly passed over for preferment, he had deserted and had later joined the Dutch East India Company. When one of its vessels, the *Grote Schur* had touched Surat on its port of call, he had jumped ship and had worked his way up north to Ahmedabad, where he had been made a platoon leader by the thakur of Narainpura, whose contingents were among those attacking Surat.

'I believe you can help in bringing this siege to a satisfactory conclusion,' said Qizl Baksh, looking up at the towering Dutchman.

'Yes, Your Excellency,' replied Vandevelde in passable Persian. 'Our cannons are too light to make any impression on the fortress walls, and the heavy artillery massed on the ramparts there are picking off our gun emplacements one by one. Somebody mentioned to me that the heavier cannon are on their way from Junagarh, but they will take too long to arrive.'

'I know the problem,' said Qizl Baksh a little testily. 'What I want is a solution.'

'Tunnels, Your Excellency. Tunnels dug underground transversely right up to the ramparts, which should then be mined. Meanwhile, to deceive the defenders, open trenches should be dug some distance away from the tunnels, so that they think that the explosives will be stacked against them from that side. The cannonading should of course continue to avoid rising suspicion.'

'Let us give it a try,' said Tufail Ahmed, one of the senior officers present. 'Nothing will be lost. Anything is better than just sitting here and firing away ineffectually at the enemy.'

Qizl Baksh thought for a moment. Then he made up his mind. 'Very well. We shall give your scheme a try and you shall be in charge of it. If you succeed, I shall personally recommend you to Prince Dara for the grant of a jagir, besides as much booty you can carry away in the sack of the city.'

The plan was put into operation in the very early hours of the next morning itself. While the digging of the open trenches was commenced with some noise and fanfare, a team of sturdy diggers was put to digging a deep well behind a screen of trees which concealed their activities from the lookouts on the fortress towers. As the open trenches approached the fortress ramparts, they were subjected to murderous punishment from the heavy guns of the defenders. Thick rhinoceros and ox hides were used to give them some sort of protective covering, but despite that, casualties among them were very high. Meanwhile, having dug a deep well, the mining party then proceeded to strike out laterally, gradually inching their way forward, unbeknownst to the defenders in the fort. Gradually, a horizontal shaft took shape, sufficient for a fully armed man to crawl through and it snaked its way well below the surface of the moat towards the fort in a zigzag fashion. Such was the secrecy maintained that the earth from the tunnel was drawn out from the pit-head only at night, in total darkness, and silently spread over the existing ground to prevent the creation of any telltale mounds visible to those in the observation posts of the fort. Eventually, late one evening, the party reached the moat and then crossed it, well below its surface, undetected by the defenders. Now they were up against the massive outer earthworks of the fort. Under Vandevelde's supervision, forty maunds of gunpowder were stacked against the wall, which took them the better part of the night, and then a very long fuse was lit.

The explosion could be heard several kos away. An enormous gap was rent in the fortress wall and hundreds of defenders, including some of Tayyib's own relatives, perished. With jubilant cries of victory, an attacking party which included Vandevelde swiftly formed and rushed through the gaping hole, sword and flaming torch in hand. Many in the assault party were killed in the initial rush, including the Dutchman. A shot from one of the defenders sitting in an embrasure hit him in the spine and he was brought out of the fort mortally wounded, where he died some hours later. However, soon the attackers were inside the fort in overwhelming numbers, swarming all over it and most of those defending it were either killed or captured. Shattered by the debacle, Tayyib sued for peace and in return for safe passage to Delhi, agreed to hand over the fort.

Qizl Baksh was ecstatic. Early next morning, in the presence of Tayyib and other notables of the fort, the great vaults of the treasury were opened and its contents were transferred on to the backs of dromedaries for their transfer to Ahmedabad. Meanwhile, all the leading merchants and moneylenders of Surat were assembled before Qizl Baksh.

'My master has the need of your assistance,' he began smoothly. 'He is embarking on a great venture to defeat the rebels and set free the Emperor, and he will succeed as surely as night follows day. Rest assured those who stand by him in this moment of need will be rewarded a hundredfold, nay thrice a hundredfold, in his hour of victory. By the same token, those who are disinclined to cooperate, will…er…a fish can hardly afford to reside in the same pool as an alligator and yet keep quarrelling with that lordly creature, can it?'

'We are perfectly willing to cooperate, My Lord, provided we know how much the impost will be,' interjected Mohammed Zahid, the headman among the traders, a gaunt, shrivelled up person, who had seen the same scene enacted several times in the past in the course of a long lifetime. His only hope was that the exactions would not be too crippling.

'Don't call it an "impost". It is only a loan. Every pie will be returned and with reasonable interest too, although our faith bars usury,' replied Qizl Baksh with a sly smile.

'Tell us how much is asked for from us, Lord, so that we can go about arranging it,' said Zahid, sick and tired of the play-acting. He knew that the assembled merchants would be lucky if they got back their principal, let alone the interest and wanted the whole thing over and done with.

'A mere trifle. Only fifty lakh rupees,' relied Qizl Baksh.

At once there were groans and cries at the size of the sum. The traders begged, pleaded, beseeched and entreated that the sum be lowered, as otherwise they would all be ruined, and none of them would be able to survive. Besides, the hostilities of the past few weeks had already disrupted trade in the town. They reminded Qizl Baksh that only a few months back, Murad had similarly ordered a raid on the treasure vaults of Surat and had practically wrung the city dry. Eventually, after hard bargaining, the sum was reduced to forty lakh rupees and this sum was advanced by Muhammed Zahid and Virji Borh on behalf of Surat's traders, in token of which they received a bond signed by Qizl Baksh, and attested with Dara's seal. The massive cannon that bristled on the outer walls of the Surat Fort were taken down to be hitched to oxen for the long journey to Ahmedabad.

'What?' cried Aurangzeb as Ghouse Mohammed, his

confidential agent in Shah Nawaz Khan's court, stood before him in his apartments in Delhi's Red Fort, nearly dropping with fatigue, having ridden practically non-stop from Ahmedabad, a week after Surat had been sacked. 'You mean to tell us that Sayyid Talib, who had pledged allegiance to us, has made over Surat and the treasure in its vaults to the minions of that infidel lover, so that he can continue to challenge our dominion?'

'I am afraid so, Your Highness,' replied Ghouse, shifting uncomfortably from one foot to another under his master's pitiless gaze as he held onto the backrest of a divan to steady himself. 'But I assure Your Highness that by all accounts it was not for any want of resistance.' Ghouse felt he must present the true picture before Aurangzeb lest he carried the impression that Talib had surrendered the fort too easily. 'All those who had returned from the Surat campaign testify that he continued to rally the defenders to the last and only capitulated when there was absolutely no other alternative available.'

'There was an alternative,' sneered Aurangzeb, clenching his teeth. 'He could have fallen on his sword, but before that, he could have taken a few infidels with him. That is what we expect our killedars to do. To fight like Ghazis and die like heroes in the cause of the true faith, rather than surrendering so tamely. You say that he is on his way to Delhi on promise of safe passage?'

Ghouse nodded uneasily.

'Well. We shall call him to account when he reaches here. We would like to know from his own lips why he values his worthless little life so precious as to be willing to surrender the fort under his charge and all that's in it to this mendacious infidel, who has turned his back on the true faith,' said Aurangzeb as his lips curled in a snarl. 'However, all that is for a later date. The intelligence you have brought us is invaluable, as it will give us time to prepare. Are you absolutely certain that our brother has decided to march northwards after linking up with Maharaja Jaswant Singh. Answer carefully for the fate of the empire may well depend upon it?'

'Yes, Your Highness. I am absolutely certain. I had this information from the governor of Gujarat Shah Nawaz Khan's personal staff. In fact, they told me that Nawaz sahib tried his level best to persuade Prince Dara to proceed to the Deccan and build up his forces there before venturing northwards, but the prince turned down that advice.'

'And that will be his undoing,' murmured Aurangzeb to himself, his eyes gleaming. 'Very well. You may go,' he said, dismissing Ghouse Mohammed with a nod. Then, beckoning an aide, he said, 'We would like to converse with Nawab Iqbal Mohammed Khan and secretary Qabil Khan straight away. Please inform them that we await their presence.'

The Nawab was the head of Aurangzeb's confidential department, while Qabil Khan was the keeper of the imperial records. Both officers were known for their outstanding ability and closeness to Aurangzeb, whom he regularly consulted whenever he was in search of the way forward.

When the officers had entered the chamber and bowed, Aurangzeb began without preliminaries. 'We have received intelligence that Sayyid Talib has handed over Surat Fort and all its treasure and heavy artillery to our brother Dara, who is now preparing to advance northwards in alliance with Maharaja Jaswant Singh in an attempt to restore the Emperor. We shall deal with Talib separately, but in the meantime, we seek your views on the way forward to forestall any attempt to restore the Emperor. In particular, we want your views on how to prise

Jaswant Singh away from any such alliance with Dara. If that were to happen, many of the other Rajput chieftains would also desert Prince Dara and he will be grievously weakened.'

'Jaswant Singh seeks to expand westwards into Jaisalmer to control the extremely lucrative trade route that passes through that territory—from the north-west of the empire right down to the Arabian Sea—to swell his coffers, Your Highness,' said Nawab Iqbal Mohammed Khan. 'In fact, it was the promise given to him by Prince Shuja of a free hand to expand towards Jaisalmer that led him to switch sides in the battle of Khajwa. It is another matter that Your Highness was victorious in that battle and the Maharaja's ambitions have been foiled for the moment. He now probably hopes that with the wealth of Surat behind him, Prince Dara might yet taste the fruit of victory and his ambition would be realized. Added to that, of course, is the age-old rivalry between the Bhati Rajputs of Jaisalmer and the Rathores of Marwar.'

'I see a way, Your Highness,' said Qabil Khan, a thin, mousy looking individual with a crafty look, who was reputed to have one of the sharpest intellects in the empire. 'Your Highness is aware that we have intercepted the delegation of Rathore nobles sent by Maharaja Jaswant Singh to Raja Prithvi Chand of Srinagar in the Garwhal Hills proposing a marriage alliance between one of the Maharaja's daughters and the Raja's son. It could be conveyed to the Maharaja that Your Highness would not stand in the way of this alliance if he gave up all plans of supporting Prince Dara, with, of course, the additional inducement that Your Highness would look the other way if the Maharaja decided to advance on Jaisalmer. Additionally, it could be given out publicly that preparations are being made to advance on Srinagar and crush Raja Prithvi Chand for daring to give refuge to Prince Sulaiman and the attack on Srinagar would be called off only if the person of the Prince is surrendered. The Maharaja could be informed in the strictest confidence that the attack would be called off only if he disavowed all plans to go to the aid of Prince Dara, so that negotiations for the marriage alliance could proceed. Elated with his success over Surat and anxious to see that Prince Sulaiman does not remain bottled up in Srinagar, Prince Dara is bound to advance deep into Hindustan to forestall any attack on Raja Prithvi Chand, confident that he has the support of Maharaja Jaswant Singh and other Rajput houses which will bring him speedily to battle at a place and time of Your Highness's choosing.'

Aurangzeb looked questioningly at Nawab Iqbal Mohammed Khan. 'Do you think this plan will work, Nawab sahib?' he asked.

I don't see why not,' replied the Nawab. 'In any case, what is the alternative? If Your Highness's accession is to be made secure, it is vital that Prince Dara's pretensions to the throne are crushed once and for all. This plan will successfully isolate him. Without Rajput support, his army will be no match for the forces Your Highness will be able to bring into the field.'

'And suppose as some sort of reinsurance, we get the Jaisalmer raja, what is his name, yes Ajai Singh, to create a little diversion on Marwar's western borders just about the time Jaswant is to join forces with our brother. That will draw the bulk of Jaswant's forces away. Ajai Singh is a mere stripling and will not suspect that he is being used as bait. Yes, I think the broad strategy is in place. Incidentally, what are your estimates of the strength of the forces that Prince Dara might bring into the field against us?'

'My agents in Ahmedabad report that there are twenty thousand foot soldiers in the barracks there, Your Highness. In addition, the mansabdars and feudatories who are still loyal to the old order can muster up another twenty thousand or so, but they would be of indifferent quality,' replied Iqbal Mohammed Khan. 'Prince Dara will perhaps consider it prudent to keep at least five thousand in reserve in case trouble breaks out while his army is on the march.'

'We can hardly associate prudence with our brother,' remarked Aurangzeb drily. 'However, do continue.'

'The foot soldiers are equipped with spears, swords, shields and arrows in sufficient numbers, but muskets are about five thousand short as also gunpowder and ball. However, it is believed that the shortage will be made up in the next two weeks or so through imports with the aid of the Portuguese.'

So, Dara was not above involving foreigners in the empire's domestic quarrels, thought Aurangzeb.

'And cavalry, Khan sahib?' he asked.

'Three thousand cavalry can be put into the field straight away, according to our reports. The smaller rajas can account for another two thousand, though the loyalty of two or three of them towards Prince Dara is doubtful and they seem to be veering towards us.'

'Who are those?'

'Bhuj, Rajkot and Radhanpur, Your Highness.'

'Do we have their representatives in court here?'

Iqbal Mohammed and Qabil Khan nodded.

'See that they are treated well,' said Aurangzeb. 'It should be made clear to them that lands, titles, high honours and jewels await them if they make a clean break with Dara and espouse our cause. By the same token have it conveyed to them that they will be mercilessly crushed if they continue to align themselves with that apostate. We do not want to dignify them by addressing them directly but have our message conveyed to them.'

'Yes, Your Highness,' the Nawab replied.

'What about elephants and camels?'

'Fifty war elephants and two hundred camels, Your Highness,' the Nawab replied.

'And ordnance?'

'After the Surat campaign, they have two hundred eight-pounders, one hundred and fifty sixteen-pounders and seventy-five thirty-two-pounders, with gunpowder and shot to match. In addition, they have three hundred swivel pieces. Some of that ordnance would still be in transit between Surat and Ahmedabad and it would take time for them to be brought upcountry.'

Aurangzeb made a quick calculation. As an experienced commander, he knew that the rate of attrition among Dara's troops would be heavy and nearly one-third of Dara's strength would be lost by the time he debouched on to the plains of Hindustan to give battle. With the imperial troops and their veteran commanders now having sworn fealty to him, Aurangzeb was confident that Dara's forces would pose no threat to him, but for victory to be assured, it was necessary to inveigle Jaswant Singh away from any attempt to support Dara.

Seven

It was a balmy morning in early spring and at the exact hour pronounced to be the most propitious by the astrologers in Dara's retinue for a campaign in a northward direction, he completed his sajda in his inner apartments and stood up. An atmosphere of expectancy hung in the still windless air, as all were waiting for him to come out of the palace. Suddenly, there was the crash of drums, the blare of trumpets, the announcement of the arrival of the heir apparent by the heralds and then surrounded by several officials, Dara emerged through the ornate doorway and slowly walked down the pillared hall to where Shah Nawaz Khan and the nobles were standing. Outside the walls of the Ahmedabad Fort, Dara's army was massed, ready to be led out for the campaign, while in the great quadrangle within the palace at the edge of the high plinth of the Diwan-e-Aam stood Siphir and some of Dara's leading generals.

Shah Nawaz Khan led Dara and the others in a procession to where Siphir stood. There, a qazi, grave and solemn, turning towards Mecca, raised both arms high in the air and recited the Fatiha. Then, lifting the lid of a case which lay on a table close by, he drew out a specially consecrated sword that rested in its scabbard and reverentially handed it to Dara.

'May this sword of righteousness prevail against all,' he intoned.

Dara grasped it with both hands, raised it to his lips and forehead and then girded it onto his waist. Then, intensely moved, in an impulsive gesture, he held Shah Nawaz Khan by both his shoulders and drew him towards his chest, embracing him tightly. 'We shall never forget all that you have done for us,' he said brokenly, tears welling up in his eyes. 'In some of our darkest moments, you have stood by us steadfastly and we are grateful to you from the bottom of our hearts for your unflinching loyalty to the Emperor.'

Shah Nawaz Khan, too, was overcome with emotion. Grasping Dara's right hand with both of his own, he bowed and then raised it to his lips and then to his forehead. 'May you prosper in all your endeavours, Your Highness, and may righteousness triumph,' he said in a choked voice.

Then Dara, followed by Siphir, ran down the steps of the Diwan-e-Aam to a gilded and highly decorated chariot for the short journey till the outer gates of the fort where their elephants stood. Watched by the townspeople of Ahmedabad who had gathered in their thousands to see their prince ride out with his army, Dara turned around to cast a last look at Shah Nawaz Khan and the other palace officials standing forlornly at the head of the Diwan-e-Aam. Then, he leapt into the chariot, followed by his son. As his captains closed in around him in strict order of precedence, the cavalcade marched out of the Ahmedabad Fort.

Their route lay through Patan, Deesa, Sirohi, Jalore and thence to Ajmer, where Jaswant Singh was expected to rendezvous with them and the combined forces were then to march on to Agra to rescue the Emperor. It was a distance of nearly six hundred kos, something which Dara's ancestor Akbar, leading a thousand crack troops in a similar journey from Agra to Ahmedabad, had performed with astonishing speed in less than eleven days nearly a century earlier. However, now weighed down with his siege train and his womenfolk, and the huge number of hangers-on that formed the complement of any Mughal army on the march, Dara knew he would be lucky if he could grapple with Aurangzeb before the torrid heat of the North Indian summer set in. More worrying for him was the fact that the loyalty of the chieftains of many of the principalities through which he would be passing on the way to Delhi was doubtful. Individually, of course, they would be no match for his army, but in case they banded together, his progress would be delayed and he would not find himself secure till Jaswant Singh's legions joined him.

The cultivators who were out in the fields that morning saw the army marching past them in an endless file like some gigantic snake, blotting out the sun with the huge swarms of dust that they were raising, with only the odd palm tree studding the landscape that was visible. On and on the army seemed to move, with pipers, drummers and flute players surrounded by the bearers of Dara's insignia out in front, playing a medley of tunes, followed by phalanxes of armed men, some on horseback while others were on foot led by their generals. Behind them came the gaily caparisoned elephants carrying Dara and Siphir—some with closed howdahs carrying the high-born ladies of Dara's entourage and others with open howdahs bearing noblemen. There were palanquins borne on the shoulders of sturdy bearers singing a dull, monotonous refrain. Bullock carts and camels followed them and then came the hangers-on, trudging on foot. Finally, tired of watching this display of martial strength, the locals returned to the performance of the immemorial tasks of rural life.

In time, the signs of habitation began to be less frequent, the fields with their standing crops shimmering in the heat haze receded into the background and the landscape became progressively drier. Mile after mile, the army trudged through practically trackless wastes, interspersed with occasional rocky outcrops and many who had commenced the march with great enthusiasm fell away, unable to bear the privations of the journey. Save for the stray thorn bush and keekar trees, there was scarcely any vegetation to break the barren, featureless landscape and the availability of water was always a serious problem. Each night at a prearranged location, carefully reconnoitered by advance elements of Dara's entourage, a halt was called and a whole tented city sprang up, all in concentric circles, with Dara and the immediate family members at the centre, and his generals, noblemen, palace officials and the troops spreading outwards in strict order of precedence, and the hordes of hangers-on who still clung to the main body like limpets, banished to the outermost fringes. Pathways were laid out between the rows of tents and watered to keep down the dust, and barricades were raised at regular intervals to control the ingress and exit and were patrolled by guards who had orders to cut down any intruder instantly.

Late one night, near the little town of Deesa, when the great camp was finally enveloped in silence except for the cries of the guards, and the occasional raucous bark of a dog, sleep eluded Nadira as she lay by Dara's side. She kept tossing and turning and finally could supress her restlessness no longer. She nudged Dara gently.

'What is it?' he murmured sleepily.

'Dearest, are you absolutely sure that Maharaja Jaswant Singh will join forces with you in the assault on Agra?'

By now, Dara was fully awake. Indeed, the same question had been gnawing at him ever since he had left Ahmedabad, but he had kept his doubts to himself. 'Why do you ask?' he queried, raising himself on his elbow and turning towards her. 'What makes you think he won't?

'I hope I am wrong, but—' just then a harsh, rasping cough overtook her. Dara had noticed this cough and also the sharp drop in Nadira's weight but had put it down to the heat and dust and the strains of the journey. Nadira went to the surahi that stood in a corner, helped herself to a goblet full of water and when the bout of coughing had ceased, continued. 'As I was saying, I hope I am wrong, but I am not sure of Jaswant Singh's fidelity to the imperial cause. The maids who bring the water for my bath were telling me that there are rumours in the camp that Maharaja Jaswant Singh may be using the coming conflict between yourself and Aurangzeb as a diversion to plan an expedition on his own to expand his territories. In which direction, they do not know and these may, of course, be just wild rumours, but you know that some of these servants have their ears much closer to the ground than us and have sources of information which are unknown to us.'

'I must confess that I have had my doubts too, but an expedition on his own? Where? We have already assured him of a free hand if he joins us against the Bhati Rajputs of Jaisalmer, with whom these Rathores have a long-standing feud, once Aurangzeb is removed from the scene. He has given us his solemn pledge to do so along with all his troops as he claims that he has several accounts to settle with our brother. His own envoy Zorawar Singh is riding with us in our suite and has confirmed more than once that the Maharaja would join forces with us. Remember also that his niece Munnwar Bai is married to our son Sulaiman, which is an added reason why he will support us.'

'It is precisely that relationship that causes me concern,' replied Nadira. 'Sulaiman has been enjoying Raja Prithvi Chand's hospitality since the last few months, but you yourself tell me that he has not been able to persuade the Raja to lend him troops so that he could attack Aurangzeb. Indeed those little hill rajas seem terrified of Aurangzeb and are behaving towards him like mice before a cat. Now suppose Aurangzeb had it conveyed to Jaswant Singh that he would not molest Prithvi Chand or Sulaiman in Garhwal, provided he cut off all links with you. Would that not give Jaswant Singh enough cause to hang back, out of love for his niece, whom he would not like to see come to any harm, if not anything else, in the coming conflict?'

'Well, I must admit that I had not looked upon it in that way, but I shall speak to Zorawar Singh first thing tomorrow morning and probe his mind,' replied Dara.

For the rest of the night, both lay silently side by side, wrapped in their own thoughts. To Nadira, waiting for dawn to break, the words of Alima Mooltani had come to haunt her. She knew instinctively that even with the support of Jaswant Singh's Rajputs, the battle could sway either way, but without them, Dara would face a decisive defeat. This was the last chance that Dara would have to wrest the empire back from Aurangzeb's hands and set free the Emperor. Would the Alima's prophesy prove correct and Dara's reign be confined to the empire of the spirit?

Next morning, Dara stood astride his elephant sent for

Zorawar Singh. As the gigantic Ceylonese beast knelt down, a small ladder was placed along its side and Zorawar Singh clambered into the howdah helped by two of Dara's aides. Zorawar was a heavily built person, with a pair of moustaches that seemed to cover half his face.

'We sent for you Raja sahib, as certain disquieting rumours have reached us that Maharaja Jaswant Singh may be vacillating in his support for us to free the Emperor,' began Dara, coming straight to the point. 'We trust these rumours are baseless, and we continue to retain Maharaja sahib's loyalty.'

'Absolutely, Your Highness. What makes Your Highness doubt it? Only late last evening, I received a message from Maharaja sahib directing me to inform Your Highness that his army is in full readiness to march out under his command. He is only waiting for the court astrologers to pronounce the auspicious moment for it to take the field. In fact, I was just about to present myself before Your Highness with this information when I received your summons.'

'We are glad to hear that,' replied Dara. 'Indeed, we had no reason to believe these idle rumours. What you have told us renews our confidence in Maharaja sahib. We would like him to avenge his defeat at Dharmat and we would like to reiterate our promise which we have communicated to him separately by letter that we would not look with disfavour on any attempt by him to expand his territories towards Jaisalmer, once this campaign is over and the Emperor is restored onto the throne of Hindustan. In any case, those Bhati Rajputs of Jaisalmer had disobeyed our instructions to send their payments of annual tribute to us in Ahmedabad and they need to be taught a lesson.'

'I shall convey the views of Your Highness to my master

speedily,' replied Zorawar as Dara urged the mahout to halt the elephant and make it kneel. Zorawar alighted and then returned to his entourage, which was riding some distance behind.

Later that evening, when Dara and his army had halted, he broached the topic to Nadira. 'Well, I summoned Zorawar Singh earlier in the day. He has reassured me that Jaswant Singh will be true to his word and meet us with his army well before we reach Ajmer, from where we will jointly proceed forward.'

'Do not rely on these assurances,' replied Nadira acerbically. 'Send your best man to Jaswant Singh's camp to assess personally whether he is really going to march with you or he has other plans up his sleeve. There is still time, but do not tarry,' again that coughing gripped Nadira, but she supressed it so as not to alarm her husband.

'You are right,' murmured Dara. 'I shall do so immediately.'

Like many weak men, he, too, thought that sudden bursts of decision-making were an adequate substitute for calm, deliberate and resolute action. Dara clapped his hands. A servitor appeared. 'We wish to converse with Altaf Hussain. Ask him to appear before us immediately.'

The attendant bowed and withdrew.

Within the space of half a watch, Altaf Hussain appeared. He was one of Dara's most intrepid confidential agents.

'We are entrusting you with a mission of the strictest confidence on which the fate of the empire may well depend,' said Dara as the slim man of middle height stood before him. 'We have received assurances from Maharaja Jaswant Singh that he would meet us with his army near Ajmer, from where we would jointly proceed towards Agra. He has conveyed that he is ready to march with us and is only waiting for the auspicious hour to do so. However, there are rumours that the Maharaja has other plans and might renege from his plighted troth. Proceed to Jodhpur at once and report back all that you see and hear. In particular, we want to know whether the Maharaja will adhere to the word he has given to us. How soon can you proceed?'

'Within one watch, Your Highness.'

'Good. Will you take anyone else with you? Remember, the journey will be long and treacherous and perhaps it would be advisable to take a couple of men with you.'

'I shall take only one man—Brahmdeo Bhil—with me. More than one will be only a hindrance and delay me.'

Dara raised a quizzical eyebrow.

'Rest assured, Your Highness. He is absolutely loyal and has been on several such journeys with me. Moreover, he is an expert tracker and is also handy with a sword and lance. As we will be travelling for a considerable part through Bhil country, he will be useful if we are stopped on the way and asked inconvenient questions.'

'Well, take whom you will. We are interested only in the results. How soon can you report back?'

'I should be able to report back in three days' time, Your Highness.'

'Dara knew that he would be as good as his word. 'Excellent! Here, take this,' Dara said, handing over a small bag to Altaf, who peered into it. The gold coins glinted dully by the light of the setting sun.

Altaf raised it to his head and then bowed.

'Go now and godspeed. Report back all that you see and hear. Khuda Hafiz.'

As the first stars began shimmering in the night sky, Altaf and Brahmdeo were on their way, heading north-west towards Jodhpur, riding at an easy trot, Altaf a little ahead of his companion, as they did not want to tire their horses. The journey was long and any fresh mounts would be hard to come by. Both were dressed like ordinary mounted troopers of some jagirdar, hastening to obey the summons of their feudal lord. Soon, Dara's great camp receded into the background and as they rode forward, they found people singly or in groups hurrying back to reach the safe confines of the camp before night fell. Now and then, a horseman rode past with his retainers or some great noble seated on his elephant passed by returning from the day's shikar and looking down with lordly disdain at the humble villagers driving their cattle and livestock towards the camp. Occasionally, they passed a palanquin borne on the shoulders of four sturdy men, their bare backs glistening with sweat, as they pressed forward with their steady drone of voice and curious shuffling gait. Bullock and camel carts, with a dog occasionally between the rear shaft and goats for milking as well as for slaughter, and even ducks and chicken all passed by, driven towards the camp they were leaving behind.

By now, night had fallen and cultivated fields were getting sparser, and large tracts of forests, dark and forbidding, were edging close to the road. Here and there, the soft lights of wick lamps could be seen through the foliage, denoting human habitation. Mile after mile, they rode through the moonless night as forest gave way to scrub land, and occasionally past cultivated fields, with the stubble of the harvested wheat still standing. At times, the low silhouette of mud huts denoting habitation against the night sky could be detected, which the two gave a wide berth. Once or twice, the barking of dogs indicated that they had come uncomfortably close to some village, but it soon subsided. Late that night, they heard the alarm call of a chital interspersed with the honk of a sambar, which testified to the presence of a leopard close by, but they were not molested and they rode on.

As dawn broke, they drew to a halt upon reaching a small clearing, by the side of which flowed a narrow stream. Tethering their horses to a nearby tree and removing their saddles, each opened his saddlebag and drew out a wrapper containing the food they had brought along with them. Altaf's consisted of chapatis and onions, along with a piece of roasted venison, while all that Brahmdeo had brought was roasted gram. They ate in silence. Each would have gladly sacrificed his life for the other, but hobbled by the cast iron laws of religion, the thought of sharing the food they had brought never entered their minds. They washed the food down with water from the stream. Soon, they were on their way again.

It was Altaf's thick quilted coat that saved him. He was riding at a slow canter a little ahead of Brahmdeo when his horse stumbled. Leopard cubs that were being trained to stalk and wanted to cross the bush-lined path nearly grazed the horse's front hooves, and its mother, lurking somewhere in the nearby bushes, apprehending that its offspring were in danger, leapt at the horse to defend her cubs. As the great cat dug its claws into the horse's left flank and tried to seize its windpipe, its right front paw sought purchase on the horse's rump and in the process, its razor-sharp claws rent a mighty gash in Altaf's side. Brahmdeo, who was barely three yards behind, reacted in a split second. Drawing his sword, he dug his heels into his own steed's flanks. His sword arm flashed and the heavy blade cleaved a large wound just below the leopard's left ear. With a roar of pain and rage, the leopard loosened its grip on the horse's neck, but with her hind legs, which were still grazing the ground, it made yet another attempt to leap up and force the horse and the rider down. Brahmdeo, however, was ready. Wheeling his horse around, he smote yet another blow, this time behind the leopard's head, and groaning, the beast fell to the ground. So severe had been the blow that the sword was wrenched from Brahmdeo's grasp and lay embedded in the leopard's skull. The gallant animal was still not quite dead. In mortal agony, it tried to regain its feet, but Brahmdeo finished it off with his lance.

'That was close!' said Altaf, looking ruefully at his rent coat as Brahmdeo pulled his lance out of the leopard's body. For a second, Altaf's horse stood still and then folded up on its knees, its mouth frothing with blood. Great gobbets of blood were spewing out of its neck where the leopard had ruptured its wind pipe. Altaf extricated himself from beneath the horse and looked on as it breathed its last. He genuinely felt sad at the loss.

'You are not badly hurt, are you?' asked Brahmdeo.

'No. Luckily, the leopard's claws got stuck in the coat,' replied Altaf, gritting his teeth as Brahmdeo helped him peel off his torn garment. Below it his undershirt was also ripped, and the leopard's claws had raked the side of his torso where bloodied strips of flesh and skin were hanging loosely, but otherwise he was unharmed. Angry welts were beginning to form on Altaf's back. Brahmdeo tore Altaf's undergarment and using fresh mud as a poultice, made some sort of a bandage and bound the wounds with it.

'This is going to delay us,' Altaf said, clenching his teeth. 'But we will have to make the best of it.'

Loosening the horse's girth and removing the saddle, the two covered its carcass and that of the dead leopard with leaves and branches. Meanwhile, the little cubs were racing each other playfully, oblivious of the death of their mother. Altaf had half a mind to pick up at least one of them, but then he put the idea firmly out of his mind. He had an important mission to carry out and this was no time for sentimentality.

'We must find another horse soon, for otherwise we will be badly delayed,' said Altaf as they went forward, with Brahmdeo carrying the horse's saddle on his shoulder.

Taking turns at riding Brahmdeo's horse, they pressed ahead till they reached the little village of Luni as dusk was setting. By now, Altaf had lost a lot of blood and he was feeling extremely weak. The village consisted of a clutch of mud huts grouped around a narrow dirt path.

'We need to find a hakeem,' said Altaf as they entered the village and spied an old grey beard sitting on his charpoy, in front of one of the huts, smoking a hookah and swatting flies that kept settling on his body as he watched the world go by.

'You are lucky. There is no hakeem here within ten kos of this village except Hakeem Abdul Majeed, who lives in the kasai tola a little distance down the path from here on the left side,' said the old man.

Altaf and Brahmdeo hastened their steps to the hakeem's shack. Abdul Majeed was a thin, cadaverous-looking man, with watery eyes and a straggly beard. As Brahmdeo sat outside, Altaf went in and explained the nature of his injuries to the hakeem. Abdul Majeed removed the rough poultice that Brahmdeo had applied, which was now soaked with blood, washed the wound in water and then taking down some containers that stood in a row on a shelf, he made a paste from extracts of goldenrod, yarrow and turmeric and applied it on the wound, which he then bound with a strip of cloth around Altaf's torso.

'You have lost some blood, but this paste will staunch the bleeding and you should find some relief in a few hours. You can rest here for a while. You are evidently a stranger in these parts. Where are you from?' the hakeem asked.

'We are from Deesa and are on our way to Jodhpur,' said Altaf evasively. 'Incidentally, I notice that the village seems practically deserted. Where are the menfolk?'

'Have you not heard? Maharaja sahib has summoned Thakur sahib and all the able-bodied men in the pargana for war.'

A faint smile broke on Altaf's lips. He knew that the Thakur of Luni paid obeisance to the jagirdar of Beawar, who, in turn, was one of Maharaja Jaswant Singh's feudatories and the fact that the Thakur had been summoned by his overlord could mean only one thing—that Jaswant Singh was getting ready to march.

'We need to proceed to Jalore immediately and we cannot afford to tarry here. Where can we procure a good horse?' Altaf asked the hakeem.

'Most of the good horses have been commandeered by the cavalry detachments under Thakur sahib. Those that are left behind are old and lame. However, you could make inquiries in the hut that is at the end of this road.'

Altaf handed the hakeem a gold mohur and then he and Brahmdeo proceeded towards the hut. After some bargaining, they were able to procure an old, brown mare reckoned to be too old for campaigning for fifty mohurs. Altaf knew that the price was extortionate, but they could not afford to haggle beyond a point.

'Don't you think we should ride back and report to His Highness that Maharaja sahib is getting ready to march towards Ajmer?' said Brahmdeo. 'You know how anxious he is to get the good news.'

'It's better that we check up personally,' replied Altaf. 'We will never be forgiven if our report happens to be incorrect. As it is, we are only about twenty kos from Jodhpur and now that we have been able to procure another horse, we should be able to cover the distance within two watches.'

Altaf and Brahmdeo hastened their pace and completed the rest of the journey without incident. The stars were peeping out of the sky and a low moon hung in the sky as Altaf and Brahmdeo finally stood before the ramparts of Jodhpur Fort. Outside its walls there was a flurry of activity as detachments of various feudatories of the Maharaja were in their individual encampments in the broad plain facing the fort, while their masters were in the palace closeted with the Maharaja. Altaf and Brahmdeo slipped in along with a mounted detachment of the thakur of Rawatsar which was entering the fort and once they were safely inside, they peeled off and proceeded towards the city centre to look for a place where they could rest a bit and in the process collect what information they could.

'We shall meet in exactly three watches from now at this spot,' said Altaf to his companion as they stood opposite a dharamshala. 'Meanwhile, gather whatever information you can.'

Brahmdeo went inside the dharamshala, while Altaf headed in the direction of a mosque, from whose minarets he could spy above the roofs of the houses, and by whose side he knew there would be a sarai for weary travellers to rest. It was the ideal place to listen to local gossip and, in the process, useful nuggets of information could be picked up. The sarai consisted of a large enclosed courtyard with deep arched alcoves raised on a high plinth all around. The courtyard was already nearly full with pack animals and baggage that the travellers were carrying and most of the alcoves were occupied. All around, Altaf could hear the hubbub of voices—some shrill, others muted, interspersed with the shouts and cries of hawkers peddling their wares including food stuffs and water. Finding one of the alcoves at the far end of the sarai to be relatively empty, he wended his way with his horse through the crowd, hitched his horse to a railing that stood in front of the alcove, and then leaning his injured back against a pillar, paused to draw breath, as the pain from the leopard's claws was now intense. He was tempted to open the packet containing dried opium leaves which he carried with him at all times to dull the pain in case of serious injuries, but refrained from doing so this time, as he needed to keep all his wits about him.

By his side was a group of men and he could not help overhearing their conversation. By their dialect, it was clear to him that they hailed from the Amber region of Rajasthan, and their occasional references to kundan jewellery, blue pottery and Sanganeri prints made it out that they were traders who had come on their annual journey to sell their wares in the markets of Jodhpur.

'Business is down these days,' lamented one of them. 'I remember, last year at about the same time, when we were here, there was such a big demand for our wares, but this time, we will be returning with most of our goods unsold.'

'That's because times are so unsettled,' said another. 'Unless peace comes about, trade will continue to suffer. And peace will not come unless Prince Aurangzeb or Prince Dara, one or the other finally quits the field.'

'Little chance of that happening,' said the first one. 'Prince Dara's troops are barely four days' march from here, heading northwards to rescue the Emperor, while Prince Aurangzeb is believed to be massing a huge army to crush Dara once and for all.'

'That won't be an easy matter,' said the first man. 'Don't you see all the preparations around you? The city is teeming with troops of the various feudatories summoned by Maharaja sahib to join him in the aid of Prince Dara, and I tell you, these Rajputs are fearsome warriors.'

'Well, Prince Aurangzeb has his own contingent of Rajput troops and they are bound to measure steel for steel against Maharaja sahib's forces. Incidentally, I gather that our Mirza Raja Jai Singh sahib was here three days ago and left yesterday. I wonder what brought him to visit Jodhpur at this hour, when he is clearly in Prince Aurangzeb's camp and battle lines are being clearly drawn.'

'Who can fathom the actions of these great personages?' mused the eldest of the lot philosophically. 'Certainly not humble folk like us who eat our daily roti by what we earn during the day.'

At the mention of Jai Singh's name, Altaf pricked up his ears. *Jai Singh? Here, in Jodhpur? Why?* Altaf, as one of Dara's senior confidential agents, was privy to a lot of information in Dara's court, and knew that Mirza Raja Jai Singh was one of Aurangzeb's most trusted Rajput generals, whom he often employed on delicate diplomatic missions when he had to win over some disaffected or recalcitrant chieftain in Rajasthan. *Had he been specially deputed by Aurangzeb to persuade Jaswant Singh to stay out of the battle?* Altaf had no means of knowing what had transpired between the two, but from the fact that Jai Singh had stayed in Jodhpur for two whole days, Altaf surmised that the discussions must have been prolonged and intense. In any case, the information of Jai Singh's visit to Jodhpur at this juncture was of the first importance and had to be conveyed to Prince Dara as quickly as possible. But first, it was necessary to confirm that Jai Singh had, in fact, visited Jodhpur. Wincing with pain on account of his injured back, Altaf came out of the sarai and went to the dharamshala. He described Brahmdeo's features to a young man who was loitering near the entrance and gave him a few coppers to call Brahmdeo out.

'I overheard in the sarai that Raja Jai Singh of Amber was here three days ago and left yesterday,' Altaf whispered to Brahmdeo when he had come out. 'This news will have to be communicated to Prince Dara as quickly as possible, because I have a strong suspicion that Jai Singh was deputed to Jodhpur by Prince Aurangzeb to persuade Maharaja Jaswant Singh to stay out of the battle and if he does so, it will be an easy victory for Prince Aurangzeb. But first, we have to confirm that Jai Singh did come here and has since left. Let us go to Maharaja sahib's palace. You go up to one of the guards and tell him that you have a message to be delivered to Saligram Singh, a member of Jai Singh's entourage.'

'Who is Saligram Singh?' Brahmdeo asked.

Altaf grinned. 'No one. I just thought up the name on the spur of the moment.'

'I don't know who this Saligram Singh is of whom you speak, but Raja Jai Singh, along with his entourage, left Jodhpur yesterday,' said the burly guard outside Jaswant Singh's palace, whom Brahmdeo accosted.

'Are you absolutely sure?' asked Brahmdeo.

'As sure as I am that you are standing in front of me, just now. I was on guard duty at the Moti Mahal, where Raja sahib was staying with his entourage and I opened its gates for the cavalcade to ride out.'

At that moment, high up in his apartments in the Phool Mahal palace within Mehrangarh Fort, overlooking the walled city of Jodhpur, Maharaja Jaswant Singh was plunged in thought. For the umpteenth time, he read the letter addressed to him by Aurangzeb which had been carried by Raja Jai Singh.

In the name of Allah, the Most Compassionate and Merciful

Maharaja sahib,

Greetings!

We trust this letter finds you in the best of health and cheer and ever mindful of the welfare of your people.

We address you at a decisive moment in the history of Hindustan, as we have received disquieting information that you have decided to throw in your lot with our brother, who has not ceased in his futile machinations to draw his sword against us.

Beware!

You have witnessed with your own eyes the fate of one brother who challenged our dominion, and as surely as night follows day, the fate of the other will be no different.

Our armies are invincible and our writ stretches from the snowy wastes of Herat and Kandahar to the steamy jungles of Bengal. A hundred rajas bow to our will and none dare even to raise their eyes to look directly at us.

Abandon all thoughts of siding with our brother, whose cause is lost, for on that path lies nothing but destruction for you and your dynasty, and instead return to our fold.

We are prepared to pardon you for your conduct at Khajwa, and indeed to restore you to all the high honours, which you had earned by your sword in enlarging the boundaries of our empire in Hindustan. Indeed, even greater honours and more glittering prospects now await you if you rejoin our cause. Once we have tidied up affairs in Hindustan, we propose to launch a campaign deep into the Deccan right up to the point where the waters of the two seas meet, and you shall have the honour of leading it. Remember, the exploits of Raja Man Singh of Amber, one of the greatest of Rajput generals, who served our glorious ancestor, Emperor Akbar (may peace be upon him) with unswerving fealty, and whose deeds will be recounted by bards till the end of time. So, too, will your glories be sung if you rejoin us, for the house of Timur can be equally generous in forgetting and forgiving past transgressions as it in smiting its foes in war.

We hold in one hand the sword and in the other the quill, with which we are willing to restore you to the high title of Maharaja, to which you were raised by our illustrious father, the Emperor. The choice is yours as to which hand you will call upon us to use, but remember, if you compel us to use our sword arm against you, you and indeed your entire dynasty will be buried in a heap of smouldering ruins.

Our trusted general Mirza Raja Jai Singh, who is the bearer of this letter and has been given plenary powers to negotiate, will elucidate any points of detail.

For two days and nights, Jai Singh had used every argument in the book to persuade Jaswant Singh to switch sides. He had coaxed, cajoled, pleaded and even mildly threatened Jaswant Singh, painting in glowing terms the advantages of abandoning Dara's cause, subtly hinting the while that Aurangzeb would look the other way if he decided to expand his principality towards the west, but the Rathore ruler was reluctant to commit himself. He hedged and prevaricated, anxious to keep his options open. Meanwhile, preparations to march by Dara's side continued, as Rathore pride forbade even as much as a hint that Jaswant might resile from his plighted word. When the astrologers in his court finally pronounced the hour most auspicious to commence the march, advance detachments of Jaswant Singh's army streamed out of Mehrangarh Fort, heading towards the rendezvous with Dara's forces.

◦❧◦

'All the preparations...for...Maharaja sahib's troops...to...to... advance towards Ajmer had been made, Your Highness, and by the time we left...Jodhpur,' Altaf gasped. He and Brahmdeo had purchased fresh horses in Jodhpur from two troopers who were getting ready to desert and had ridden practically non-stop, straight to Lunkaran, where Dara was now encamped. While Brahmdeo had gone to his billet, Altaf now stood before his master to make his report, almost half-dead with fatigue and pain from the throbbing wound, which had begun to suppurate.

'Good God!' said Dara kindly. 'There is no such hurry. Regain your breath, collect yourself and then tell me all that you heard and saw in Jodhpur. Wait,' he signalled to an attendant, 'bring some water at once.' Then, turning to Altaf, he said, 'We see you are badly hurt. Were you attacked?'

Altaf nodded slightly. 'Only a scratch, Your Highness.' He mumbled through parched lips. 'My…horse stumbled…over two…leopard cubs and its mother, who was in the…bushes nearby attacked us. The wound was treated by…a local hakeem.'

Dara beckoned another attendant. 'Ask Hakeem Mohammed Mirza to come here immediately.'

Meanwhile, the attendant who had gone into a nearby tent, came out with a large earthen jug of water. Altaf drank from it in great gulps, and then having composed himself, continued. 'As I was submitting, Your Highness, cavalry regiments had already ridden out with the artillery a day ahead and Maharaja Jaswant Singh himself was following with foot soldiers on elephant back. He should now be about two days' march from here. The number of troops are put at around twenty to twenty-five thousand and the artillery pieces approximately fifty all told, but they consist of relatively smaller items.'

'It is not so much their artillery pieces with which we are concerned, of which we already have enough, but their mounted horsemen for the Rajput cavalry is among the most feared in battle,' said Dara exultantly. By the light of flaming torches held by attendants, outside the tent where the two now stood, Altaf could see Dara's face breaking out into an ecstatic smile at the news of Jaswant Singh's troop movements. So all the talk of him deserting the cause had been idle rumours. With Jaswant's formidable Rajput warriors on his side, Dara was confident that the two adversaries would be more evenly matched.

'There is however one point, Your Highness,' Altaf remarked.

'Yes. What is that?' asked Dara eagerly.

'Mirza Raja Jai Singh of Amber was in Jodhpur and left

the day before we reached there. He and Maharaja sahib were closeted together for two whole days. No one was privy to the discussions, but rumours gathered from members of Mirza sahib's entourage were circulating in the city that his visit was to persuade Maharaja sahib not to participate in the coming conflict on the promise of receiving high honours if he stayed neutral.'

At once, Dara's face clouded. Were these rumours correct? Had Jai Singh's mission been successful? Had all these preparations, these marching movements been a ruse, an elaborate feint to delude Dara into thinking that Jaswant was with him all along, only to deliver him at the last moment into the hands of his hated brother when the battle was actually joined? He had to know, but how? A delegation at the highest level would have to be sent to probe Jaswant Singh's intentions and make him stick to his plighted word. But whom to send? Obviously, he could not go himself, for the putative heir to the Mughal throne could not be seen as a supplicant before a Rajput chieftain. Why not send his son Siphir? Yes, that was it! He was the grandson of the Emperor, and the mission would carry sufficient weight. He would, of course, be accompanied by Zahid Khan, the grand chamberlain, Rashid Khan, the leading general in Dara's army and other high officials, who would do the talking. But the presence of Siphir, a Mughal scion, at his doorstep would certainly flatter the Rathore ruler.

Just then the royal hakeem arrived and as Altaf was led away to be treated by him, Dara went back into his tent in a thoughtful mood.

'Maharaja Jaswant Singh is marching towards us with his army,' said Dara to Nadira that night as both were preparing to retire. 'His troops will be a welcome addition when we settle final accounts with our brother, for we learn that Aurangzeb has also set out with his army and most likely the encounter will take place somewhere in the vicinity of Ajmer. However, the man I had sent to Jodhpur to find out what Jaswant's plans were, has just returned with the news that Mirza Raja Jai Singh of Amber was in Jodhpur for two days. It is rumoured that he was there at the instance of our brother to persuade Jaswant to hang back in the coming battle on the promise of high honours. Really, the mendacity of our brother has no limits. He will stop at nothing to get his way.'

'What do you propose to do?' asked Nadira with concern, as her forebodings might be coming true. Before Dara could reply, a fit of coughing overtook her. She was again seized with one of those persistent attacks of coughing, which she had tried to supress so as not to alarm her husband. This time, too, she swallowed hard and then drank water from a surahi kept close by.

'You should get your cough seen to by hakeem sahib,' said Dara. Then, seeing that it had subsided, he thought no more of it and went on, 'Well, I cannot personally go to meet Jaswant Singh, as that would dignify him beyond his station, for after all, he is only one among many Rajput chieftains. However, I propose we send Siphir with Zahid Khan and a couple of other leading generals on the pretext of coordinating the war plans before the battle ensues. They will try to probe Jaswant's final intentions. The fact that Siphir, the Emperor's grandson, is leading the mission will give it the necessary weight. Of course, most of the talking will be done by Zahid and the others. Moreover, it will give Siphir some idea of how battle tactics are drawn up which will stand him in good stead in later years.'

'I hope no harm comes to him,' Nadira said, worrying about her son's safety. 'After all, he is only a boy. Suppose he is detained by the Rajputs?'

'Don't you worry, my dearest,' replied Dara, raising her chin till their eyes met as he smiled at her. 'Remember, he smote a Deccani spearman at Samugarh, and has wounds to show for. After all, is he not our son? Moreover, he is not going to war but is only leading a diplomatic mission. As for his being detained by the Rajputs, they will not dare to face everlasting disgrace and ridicule by detaining their guest, and that too a young boy, for their standards of hospitality are legendary.'

'Do as you think best,' replied Nadira resignedly. 'Somehow, in my view, these two-day confabulations between Jai Singh and Jaswant Singh does not bode well for us. If Jaswant Singh is truly on our side, he would have sent Jai Singh packing within the hour.' As another bout of coughing was about to seize her, she drew away and drank some more water.

⌒∽⌒

Swift riders had been sent to Jaswant Singh to be ready to receive the royal party, and when Siphir and his entourage were within sight of Jaswant's camp, a grand reception awaited them. Jaswant Singh, a tall, heavily built man with a bulbous nose and protruding eyes, rode out some distance on his elephant to welcome the guests and when Siphir drew near, the huge beast was made to kneel down. A small ladder was lowered on its side, and Siphir, after dismounting from his horse, climbed into the gaily caparisoned howdah and sat by Jaswant Singh's side, while his retinue rode a little behind.

'Welcome, Shahzadeh sahib. I trust you suffered no inconvenience during the journey,' said Jaswant smilingly, turning to Siphir as the party wended its way through the throngs of cheering Rajput nobles and soldiers to Jaswant Singh's tents.

'None at all,' replied Siphir, acknowledging the greetings of the assembled troops.

Inside the main tent, refreshments were served and then the two sides got down to business.

'The latest reports indicate that Prince Aurangzeb, with his army of approximately forty-five thousand men, is somewhere between Jaipur and Ajmer and would be reaching Ajmer in ten days or so,' began Rashid Khan, Dara's leading general. 'He would obviously like the battle to be fought on open ground, far from the intervening hillocks that dot the landscape, as that would give him the advantage of exploiting the weight of numbers.'

'Mere numbers don't mean anything,' countered Jaswant dismissively. 'The bulk of his formations still consist of that Deccani rabble he brought with him from his viceroyalty. One of my men is equal to ten of them.'

'Well, they certainly showed their mettle at Dharmat,' remarked Zahid Khan, the grand chamberlain, drily, wanting to keep the Rathore ruler off balance.

At the mention of Dharmat, Jaswant bristled and with difficulty kept his composure. 'Prince Aurangzeb's victory on that battlefield was because the ground was wet after the previous night's rainfall and on the one side was marshland, while on the other, a series of ditches. There was absolutely no room for my cavalry to manoeuvre. Here, the situation is different. The ground is hard and crisp and there is plenty of scope to mount attacks from the flanks.'

'I propose that after the initial exchange of artillery fire, instead of clashing with the enemy head-on, we draw them in towards us, under the impression that we are retreating as a result of their artillery barrage,' countered Rashid Khan. 'They will then rush in with their cavalry to try and pierce our centre followed by their foot soldiers and then turn outwards to defeat our detachments in detail, at which point Maharaja sahib's cavalry units, which could be in readiness on either side of the battlefield, could gallop forward, along their flanks wheel around and envelop the enemy from the rear.'

'I have an even better idea,' remarked Jaswant. 'In fact, I propose to employ the tactics of double encirclement. 'While some units of my cavalry will envelop the enemy from the flanks—as suggested, reserves will be unleashed in a wider arc so that any retreating soldiers are caught in the outer ring and not allowed to escape. They will surely be annihilated.'

To illustrate his tactic, Jaswant drew two sweeping arcs with the point of his sword on the priceless carpet on which they were standing. The arcs commenced from the flanks of the battlefront and met well behind the enemy lines.

Throughout the day, the battle tactics were discussed and by the time Siphir and his party were finally ready to return to their camp, a rough plan had been worked out supplemented by Jaswant Singh's own suggestions. Despite Jaswant's protestations, Rashid Khan was not entirely convinced that when the battle actually commenced, Jaswant would act in the manner he had promised and if he sat aside, Rashid Khan knew that several other Rajput rulers would follow. However, the wily general kept his thoughts to himself.

☙❧

'We had a useful council of war,' said Rashid Khan as he stood before Dara to make his report and explain what had been decided upon. 'Maharaja Jaswant Singh was his usual expansive self and fell in with the tactics suggested including his own refinement of employing the tactics of double encirclement, that is while some units of his cavalry would engage the enemy from the flanks, the other echelons would sweep forward, wheel around and attack from the rear to kill or capture any stragglers. The enemy will be pressed in among themselves and will not be able to bring to bear their superiority of numbers.'

'Well, that is splendid!' beamed Dara. 'We knew that Maharaja sahib would not let us down. That warrior race stands by their word and to them, their word is truly their bond.'

'I will believe the Maharaja only when I see his troops actively engaging the enemy on the battlefield,' replied Rashid Khan drily.

'Why so?' asked Dara, sounding a bit surprised. 'What doubts can you possibly have? Jaswant Singh has given his word and is bound to stick to it. Moreover, he wants to avenge his defeat at Dharmat and that should give him cause enough to join us in battle against Aurangzeb.'

'I don't know, Your Highness, but somehow I feel that we should not rely on Jaswant Singh's support.'

'We think you are being unduly pessimistic,' said Dara. 'You will see that when the battle is joined, he will be standing four-square with us. We have now to locate a battlefield where the tactics you have decided upon can be exploited to the greatest advantage.'

⌒◯◯⌒

As Dara's army pressed northwards, scouts scoured the surrounding countryside to locate a suitable battleground that Dara knew would decide not only his own fate but that of the Mughal empire in Hindustan. Finally, the scouts reported on the existence of a broad plain stretching nearly three kos on either side and completely featureless except for a few keekar and babool trees, which would give ample scope for manoeuvre. Dara and his generals hastened to the spot.

'This will be the ideal site to offer battle,' said Rashid Khan and Zafar Khan as they approached the plain, deciding which was the best place to make their stand. 'The enemy will try and attack us in the vicinity so that we are as far from Delhi and Agra as possible. Besides, the ground is hard and crisp, with plenty of scope for manoeuvre. Once the rebels come into sight, there will be the initial exchange of artillery, and then, we will make it appear as if we are withdrawing. We will lead the enemy cavalry and their foot soldiers on to us and when the enemy are amidst us, employ the double encirclement tactics that Jaswant Singh has spoken about.'

'Yes, this field is as good as any,' said Dara eagerly, excited that it was now only a question of when before he came to grips with his hated bother and delivered a blow from which he would never recover. He dropped camp in a little copse of trees on the edge of the plain, and riders were sent out to apprise Jaswant Singh of their location and escort them to the imperial camp.

When after waiting for two whole days, there was no sign of Jaswant Singh's advance scouts, the first glimmerings of doubt began to creep into Dara's mind. Had Jai Singh's persuasion worked? Had Jaswant decided to break his pledged word? Had his professed loyalty to the Emperor been merely a mask behind which he would pledge his sword to the highest bidder?

'Why is there no news of Jaswant's movements so far?' asked Dara, lines of worry creasing his face.

'Our riders went out two days ago, Your Highness,' replied Rashid Khan. 'This silence on Maharaja sahib's part seems ominous.'

Just then there was some commotion in the outer perimeter of Dara's camp. A mounted Rajput trooper could be seen trying to enter the camp and being forcibly made to dismount. Then after being disarmed and escorted by two hefty guards, he was brought to one of the outlying tents within Dara's camp as a court official ascertained the purpose of his mission. He was then passed on to the court chamberlain, who took him under guard to Dara's tent, where he was made to wait.

The court chamberlain went inside. 'A messenger has come from Maharaja Jaswant Singh. He bears a message for Your Highness,' he said.

'Maharaja sahib has entrusted me with this message to be handed over to His Highness,' said the trooper as he drew out a cylinder from his tunic which he handed over to the chamberlain.

The chamberlain opened its lid and drew out a piece of rolled parchment, which he handed over to Dara, who unrolled it. As he ran his eyes over its contents, his worst fears were confirmed.

Your Highness,

The Rathore Dynasty of Marwar has never failed in its loyalty to the house of Timur and has shed its precious blood to help plant the Mughal flag in distant lands. Indeed, in recognition of the contribution of the Rathore Dynasty in the expansion of the boundaries of the Mughal empire, His Majesty the Emperor was pleased to ennoble your humble servant with the title of Maharaja.

It was the life's ambition of this humble servant of yours to join forces with your army, avenge the defeat at Dharmat, vanquish the usurper and set right the monstrous wrong committed on His Majesty the Emperor by restoring him onto the throne of Hindustan, but fate often plays a cruel hand and circumstances arise when the most pious intentions have to be set aside in the face of stern realities.

I have received word that hoping to profit from the present distraction that afflicts the region, the Bhati Rajputs, under Raja Ajai Singh of Jaisalmer, have crossed the border and invaded Marwar with a large army. At moments like this, it is my bounden duty as a ruler to rush to the defence of my realm and protect my people.

I am therefore proceeding to repel this invasion and as soon as the enemy has been dealt a blow from which he will never recover, this sword of mine, will once again be unsheathed in the cause of righteousness which Your Highness so vividly exemplifies.

'Where are the Maharaja's troops now?' Dara asked the trooper harshly. He was hoping against hope that the Maharaja was not too far away and a swift rider could still be sent to appeal to him to return.

'Maharaja sahib left with the cavalry detachments two days ago and ordered the other detachments to follow,' replied the trooper. 'They will be at least forty kos from here.'

Despair was writ large on Dara's face, for he knew that the chances of Jaswant Singh returning to the campaign before battle with Aurangzeb was joined were minimal. When his own frontiers were threatened, would not Jaswant first rush to repel the invader? Without Jaswant's troops, Dara knew that his own forces would be hopelessly outnumbered and out in the open country, where he had chosen to give battle, they would be decimated within the hour. Frantic with concern, he sent for his generals Rashid Khan and Zafar Khan.

'Maharaja Jaswant sahib will not be joining us,' Dara intoned in a low voice, which was barely a whisper as the two generals stood before him. 'He has just informed us by a courier that his western border has been breached by Raja Ajai Singh of Jaisalmer and he has proceeded to repel the invasion. He, of course, promises to return after defeating the Raja, but that is no solace, as battle will be joined well before that. We will have to rely on the forces we have. If we decide to fight our brother in the open country here, we are sure to be outnumbered and defeated. We seek your opinion on the course of action we should follow.'

'We have to select a spot to give battle where the larger numbers of the enemy gives him no advantage,' replied Rashid Khan. If I am permitted to make a suggestion…'

'Yes, yes, go on,' said Dara a little testily, growing impatient by the minute.

'If he is to attack us here, Prince Aurangzeb will have to cross Ajmer and traverse through the pass at Deorai, which lies at the head of a narrow valley in the Aravalli Hills. I would humbly suggest that we take up defensive positions in and around the pass. It should be possible to hold him there with the far fewer numbers that we presently have, and the hilly terrain will render his cavalry largely immobile. Moreover, if we dominate the heights above the pass, their artillery will be relatively ineffective and their gun crew can be easily picked off by our matchlock and bowmen as they come up the valley to try and dislodge us. If we can hold them for a sufficiently long period at the pass, there is a strong chance that other Rajput and Jat principalities in the region will join our cause.'

Dara looked at Zafar Khan with a questioning glance. What is your opinion?' he asked.

'Khan sahib's suggestion seems eminently practical,' he answered. 'In any case, what alternative do we have?'

'How far is this pass from here?' asked Dara.

'It's about four kos south of Ajmer, Your Highness. With the guns and the other paraphernalia, it would take about four days for us to reach there.'

'And Prince Aurangzeb? How far away is he on the opposite side of it?'

'The latest reports indicate that his speed is impeded by his heavy guns as his artillery chief, Saif Shikan Khan, has not been able to procure enough draught oxen to haul them and are relying on the war elephants to do so. Our own estimation is that it will take at least nine days for the rebel forces to reach the pass.'

'What about the ladies? We have to ensure their safety,' asked Dara.

'They can halt near Ana Sagar Lake some distance away from Deorai, Your Highness. After the battle is over, they can be escorted to the pass. They will be safe near the lake.'

'Very well. We shall go by your advice, as we realize that there is no other alternative available.'

Later that evening, Dara broke the news to Nadira. 'Jaswant Singh will not be joining our forces. His western border has been attacked by Ajai Singh of Jaisalmer and he has gone to defend his throne. I shall be proceeding with the army to the pass near a place called Deorai, which my generals tell me is the best place to hold Aurangzeb, as he will have to pass through it if he wants to attack us. You and the other ladies of the court will remain near the Ana Sagar Lake, which is some distance away from the pass, and will join us after Aurangzeb is sent scuttling back.'

Nadira said nothing. If only what Dara was saying came true.

Meanwhile, away to the north, in Aurangzeb's camp, there was jubilation. Through his spies, he had been getting up-to-date reports of the movements of his adversaries, and late one night when one of his spies was brought to his tent and gave him the information that Jaswant Singh had pulled away from Dara's forces to tackle Ajai Singh, who had invaded his western border, Aurangzeb's face broke into a smile. His plan was working perfectly, for it was he who had prompted Ajai Singh to seize the opportunity and expand eastwards with promises of accretion of Marwar territory, knowing fully well that Jaswant Singh would rush to the defence of his kingdom.

Eight

The pass at Deorai is nestled between two hills of the Aravalli Range and having decided to make their stand there, Dara's forces prepared to hasten to the spot to reconnoitre the area and select the defensive positions they would take in the narrow valley that the enemy would have to negotiate to reach the pass. The guns were once again yoked to the oxen, the bivouacs of the troops were dismantled; the tents and pavilions were brought down and loaded, and the elephants, horses, camels and mules were once again got in readiness to proceed to the site, where the fateful encounter was to take place. Upon reaching the pass, Dara approved the site for the ensuing battle.

Several trees on both sides of the valley slope were cut down to make way for gun emplacements, which were then hauled into position by local tribal villagers, who led a precarious existence in little hutments in the valley and who were dragooned on pain of death for the purpose. The guns were concealed with brushwood, and so positioned as to command a field of fire along the length of the valley. Sacks of gunpowder, cannonballs and naphtha were then stacked close to the guns and the gun crew were ordered to sleep at their positions. Embankments were raised and trenches were dug, behind which the foot soldiers awaited the commencement of hostilities, while matchlock-men and bowmen were positioned behind boulders, large rocks, trees and whatever cover was available to tackle the enemy at close quarters when they approached. Lookouts were posted on all the hilltops to report the movements of the enemy troops. After the preparations to face the assault had been made, as the hours ticked by, all that remained was to wait.

Early one morning on the third day of having reached the pass, a lookout posted on the highest point of the hill overlooking the plain, across which Aurangzeb's forces were to advance, spotting a cloud of dust, ran down the rocky slope as fast as his legs could carry him and reached the outer perimeter of the enclosure within which stood the tents of Dara and his leading generals. Escorted by two burly guards, he was led to Dara's tent.

'The enemy, Sire...it has been sighted,' he gasped.

'Where?' asked Dara.

The scout pointed in an easterly direction.

'Quick,' said Dara to the generals who were assembled around him.

Hastily, they rose and accompanied the lookout up the steep slope to the post.

Aurangzeb had reached Deorai the previous day and had dropped camp on the edge of the plain some two kos east of the pass. Now below them, through the dust haze in the distance, Dara could see Aurangzeb's army in full panoply wheeling into position in the traditional Mughal order of battle. Some distance ahead of the army rode the scouts, while the artillery was drawn up in front with gaps between the guns for the foot soldiers to rush through. Behind them stood the vanguard with the two wings of the heavily armed shock cavalry on either sides of it and echeloned behind them were units of the light cavalry, which would be ordered into battle to deliver the coup de grâce. Behind the van stood the advanced reserve which would rush to the aid of either flank in case it was hard-pressed and behind them all was Aurangzeb himself, on his gigantic Ceylonese elephant, with a commanding view of the entire battleground, surrounded by his fanatically loyal household troops interspersed with matchlock-men, swordsmen, pikemen and archers.

As the enemy troops drew near, a frisson of excitement swept through the defenders. The hour of reckoning was finally at hand. Would they be able to repel the onslaught?

When Saif Shikan Khan, the commander of Aurangzeb's artillery forces, felt he had come within range, he rode up to Aurangzeb and sought permission to open fire.

Aurangzeb nodded and the first volley of gunfire shattered the stillness of the morning. When the smoke cleared, it was noticed that the firing had done little damage to the defenders, as the trajectory of the cannonballs was not high enough to destroy Dara's gun emplacements positioned in the hillsides and the projectiles reached only the lower reaches of the valley. Edging the cannon further up, another sustained barrage was let loose, but the results were much the same, as the cannonballs still could not reach Dara's artillery and his troops higher up on the hillsides.

Dara was exultant on seeing the failure of Aurangzeb's artillery to make any impact. He ordered his own artillery to respond and the huge thirty-two-pounders, hauled all the way from Surat with a far greater range and now positioned with back-breaking effort in the sides of the valley, fired a murderous volley at the guns below. One cannonball tore off the barrel of an opposing cannon from its carriage and set the sacks of gunpowder that were stacked close by on fire. Screaming in pain, the gun crew, their bodies aflame, tried to bolt, but the line of guards standing close by pushed them back at the point of their swords.

Meanwhile, as the artillery duel was progressing, Aurangzeb's cavalry had wheeled into position. Baffled by the failure of his artillery to silence Dara's guns, Aurangzeb ordered his cavalry into battle. As they charged forward with levelled lances and flashing swords across the plain, Dara's artillery tore great gaps in their ranks, but still they came on like a surging tide. However, once they reached the mouth of the narrow valley, their momentum slackened. The limited confines made several horsemen jostle against each other and those with an uneasy grip were unseated and trampled underfoot by the slashing hooves of the horses coming behind. Meanwhile, several horses slithered and slid on the rough, rocky surface of the valley, which in times past had been the bed of a rivulet, as their hooves could not find enough purchase to sustain the momentum of the charge. A few managed to reach the lowest of the breastworks and with lance and sword stabbed at those who were sheltered behind it, but a few well-aimed arrows from the archers who were hiding in the trees brought them down.

Again and again, with blood-curdling cries the cavalry hurled themselves on the defenders, but were repulsed by accurate fire coming from Dara's matchlock-men and archers.

'We will have to send in the foot soldiers if we are to dislodge the enemy, Your Highness,' said Bahadur Khan, sweat pouring from his face as he rode up to Aurangzeb, who by now had advanced closer to the mouth of the valley to watch the operations.

'Yes, do so,' shouted Aurangzeb atop his elephant. 'We shall see how long these infidel lovers can withstand our wrath.'

In a great tide, the foot soldiers rushed forward through the gaps in the guns and tried to storm the entrenchments in the lower reaches of the valley, but were stopped in their tracks by the defenders, who stood up and let loose a murderous volley. The attackers recoiled; many stumbled and fell to be trampled by those coming behind and their groans and cries of agony rent the air.

Throughout the day, Aurangzeb pressed forward his attacks, but Dara's carefully chosen defensive positions gave him a priceless tactical advantage and each assault made by Aurangzeb's foot soldiers was blunted. When darkness fell on the blood-soaked valley floor and hostilities ceased, Dara was exultant that he had successfully repelled Aurangzeb's ferocious assaults, while Aurangzeb was at his wits' end as to how he could bring the battle to a successful conclusion.

The next morning, the battle resumed, but the results were no different. While Dara's defensive position could not be overwhelmed by the attacking forces, he knew that he did not have the offensive capability to drive Aurangzeb back. Yet, both were aware that if Aurangzeb did not win, it would be a defeat for him, while if Dara were not defeated, victory would be his. Meanwhile, the corpses were piling up on the valley floor and were beginning to emit a foul, putrid stench. For Aurangzeb, the stalemate somehow had to be broken.

On a hilltop overlooking the valley was a small village of some fifteen thatched and mud hutments inhabited by members of the Kolari tribe, who eked out a precarious living by petty thievery and by collecting wild honey from the flowers that grew on the slopes of the valley and selling it in the city of Ajmer. Chitvan was a young boy of seventeen, belonging to that tribe, who looked somewhat older than his years, and from his hiding place high on the hilltop, he had been furtively watching the struggle in the valley below. In his visits to Ajmer city to sell his honey, he had seen the soldiers of one chieftain or another swaggering about, entering shops and taking what they wanted without paying for them and roughly brushing aside the entreaties of the terrified shopkeepers. He admired their weapons and the clothes they wore and it was his life's ambition to become like one of them. Late in the evening of the second day of battle, after hostilities had ceased, he thought he saw his chance. Why not go down to the entrenchments and offer to work for the troopers? Perhaps in time, they would accept him as one of them. With an earthen pot full of honey, he went down the hillside by a steep and narrow footpath, in his dirt-stained, ragged clothes and approached the nearest entrenchment, where Dara's men were resting from the exertions of the day's battle. Some were cleaning their weapons for the next day's hostilities that were sure to commence, while others, amidst groans and cries, were tending their wounds.

'Masters, see this fresh honey,' Chitvan cried out when he got close to the entrenchment, employing, with practised ease the skills with which he sold his wares in the streets of Ajmer. 'It is sweeter than nectar from heaven. One taste of it and it will transport you to paradise. Surely, my masters would not have tasted anything like it.'

'Come here, boy,' said the leader of the troop in the nearest entrenchment, taking in Chitvan's dishevelled appearance with no little disgust, but at the same time anxious to sample the young man's wares. 'Let's see what you have with you.'

Chitvan went forward hesitantly and then halted. 'Master,

this delicious honey is yours, for which you need make no payment if you allow me to work for your men here,' he said.

'Let us first see what you have,' said the leader roughly as he snatched the pot from the young boy's hands. He opened the lid and dipped his knife into it, drew it out and then wiped his finger onto its blade, which he then took to his mouth.

'Mmmm. This is good,' he said as he dug in more fully and then passed the pot around to the others. In a trice, the pot was empty and the last trooper had plunged his hand into the pot to draw out the remnants.

'Master, you will permit me to join your men, won't you?' Chitvan asked, looking at then expectantly.

'Be off with you now,' said the leader roughly. 'War is serious business and the trench can't be dirtied by low-caste, filthy scums like you.'

'Let the boy come into the trench,' said another trooper, taking pity on Chitvan. 'He can at least clean the muck around here. Who knows, he can even have a shot at the enemy, and if he gets his brains blown out, well that is his fate. After all, he was the one who came asking for it.'

'None of it,' the leader retorted. 'We can't have filthy scums like him in our trenches.'

'Please, Master. I beg of you. I promise I will obey you,' Chitvan said, looking pleadingly at the trooper, who seemed to be inclined in his favour, but that man nodded his head towards the leader.

'Will you be off now or should we kick you out?' the leader threatened.

'At least pay me for the honey,' cried Chitvan, disappointment welling up inside him now that his plan to enlist had gone so horribly wrong.

'You dare to ask us for money, you miserable son of a whore,' cried the leader standing as if to strike the boy. 'Get out of here this instant or you will not live to see another day.' He dropped the pot, which shattered into smithereens and advanced towards Chitvan with drawn sword, who fearing that he would be assaulted, ran back the way he had come, his tearful face contorted with rage and humiliation. *Dirty scum?* Well, he would show them and they would regret it for the rest of their lives. Now more than the desire to fight as a trooper, it was the baleful spirit of revenge that had overtaken him. Then a thought struck him. He swiftly descended the slope and made his way towards Aurangzeb's camp, whose fires spread across the plain twinkled in the night.

As he approached the lines, he was accosted by a burly guard. 'Take me to your master,' Chitvan said with as much authority as he could muster, although in his heart he was quaking. 'I have information that might be useful to him.'

Accompanied by two guards with drawn swords who were ready to cut him down at the least untoward movement, he was taken up the hierarchy till he stood before Bahadur Khan, who had come out of his tent.

'Master, I know a secret path which will get you behind the enemy lines,' Chitvan said.

Aurangzeb's commander looked keenly at the young boy. Was he telling the truth? Was there indeed such a path, or was it a trap? If such a path really did exist, it could shorten the battle appreciably. But should he take such a decision at his own level? Better not, he decided, for if it went wrong, he would not be forgiven. Under Aurangzeb, there were no second chances. 'Come with me,' he ordered.

He took Chitvan to Aurangzeb's tent, which stood some

distance away in a heavily guarded enclosure.

'This young man says that he knows a secret path by which the enemy's front could be turned, Your Highness,' said Bahadur Khan, addressing Aurangzeb, who had emerged out of his tent.

'Who are you? Where do you live?' asked Aurangzeb, fixing Chitvan with his keen eyes.

'I live on the crest of the hill there, Sire,' replied Chitvan, pointing to the hutments high above and behind him. 'Our tribe consists of honey tappers. We collect and sell honey in Ajmer. I have spent my entire life here and have climbed these hills collecting honey. I am familiar with every rock and boulder here. I know a secret path by which Your Lordship can get behind the enemy entrenchments.'

'He seems to be speaking the truth, Your Highness. Perhaps we can get him to show us this path that he speaks of. We will get the opportunity to outflank the enemy and hit them in the rear. In any case, nothing will be lost and it is better than another frontal assault which is getting us nowhere,' said Bahadur Khan.

Aurangzeb thought for a moment and then agreed. 'You are right,' he said. 'Send a strong detachment of frontline soldiers, armed with matchlocks, bows, swords and pikes along with this boy up the path he is going to show us, if indeed there is such a path, and when the troops reach a point behind the enemy lines when they are poised for attack, let them light a flare so that the attack from the rear can be coordinated with a frontal assault up the valley.' Then turning to Chitvan he added, 'Remember, boy, if you are telling lies and if this is a trap, you will be cut down instantly and your tribe will be shown no mercy. You will be closely watched every step of the way, but if this secret path does exist as you say it does and the attack succeeds, you and your entire tribe will be well-rewarded.'

The plan was put swiftly into operation. The night was dark and moonless as a heavily armed shock detachment of veteran troopers were assembled for the climb up the path and then for attack from the rear. Then as Chitvan walked with swift loping strides ahead, the troopers strung along behind him, in twos and threes and sometimes in a single file when the path became too narrow. In time, they left behind the dying fires of Aurangzeb's camp and by a wide, circuitous route found themselves at the base of a gorge running approximately parallel to the one in which the battle was being fought, with sides so steep as to be almost perpendicular. A thin, narrow pathway, almost like a ribbon, effectively concealed by trees and bramble, snaked up the further side of this gorge and ended in a saddle, which provided access to the range below, from which the rear of Dara's tents, gun emplacements and trenches could be seen.

Encumbered by their weaponry and the narrowness of the path they were treading, the detachment made their slow, painful progress towards the saddle. Two of the soldiers lost their footing as the stem of some plants on the side of the hill they were clutching onto in order to save themselves came away in their hands. With a scream they went crashing down, their lifeless bodies lying spread eagled on the rocks below.

'Steady on, steady on,' whispered the captain of the detachment harshly to those who were following behind. Finally, the detachment reached the start of the saddle, from where the going was relatively easier. Assembling at a point which overlooked Dara's encampment, they lit flares which were visible to Aurangzeb's troops at the far end of the valley.

Meanwhile, Aurangzeb had been keenly watching the crest of the hill from where the attack on Dara's rear was to commence. The troops for the frontal assault had already been put into position and were primed and ready.

The moment he saw the flares being waved on the crest, he cried, 'Now, Khan sahib.'

While on Bahadur Khan's orders the frontline troops hurled themselves forward with blood-curdling cries and flashing swords, those who were on the crest of the hill poured down its slope to attack Dara's rear, whose troops could not realize what hit them.

'We are surrounded,' cried one. 'Run for your lives,' cried another. Some emerged groggily from their entrenchments only to be cut down by the attackers, who swarmed all around them.

Dara was asleep in his tent when an attendant rushed in. 'Awake, Sire, and hurry,' he shouted. 'The enemy has surrounded us from all sides. Unless you leave this instant, you will be captured.'

Dara hurriedly rose from his bed and awakened Siphir, who was sleeping by his side. He emerged out of his tent in his night dress and slippers and looked about him. The sight filled him with horror. All around him there was tumult, chaos and confusion. Smoke and dust made even objects close by difficult to see and shouts and cries filled the air. Tents and bivouacs were being torn down and were aflame, and in their lurid lights, through the haze, Dara could see Aurangzeb's soldiers who had attacked from the rear slashing away at his own personal guards in their pickets, who were scrambling to offer some resistance, while further down the valley, his troops were trying to stem the frontal assault.

'Where is that infidel lover?' snarled the captain of the detachment, followed by his men as they went from one tent to the other looking for Dara, tearing away the tent cloth and stabbing at anything that moved as they rushed past.

Dara knew that if he delayed even for a moment, all would be lost. Before the attackers could reach his tent, he grabbed his sword and taking advantage of the darkness, he and Siphir hastened to where the horses were tethered and followed by a few of their personal guards, they sped towards Ana Sagar Lake, where Nadira and the other ladies of the court had been anxiously waiting since noon for news of the battle. With the ladies was Dara's treasure, which was guarded by his faithful eunuch Khwaja Maqbool .

For Dara now, half-crazed with worry, it was vital that the security of the ladies be ensured before any plans could be devised for overcoming the debacle. When he and Siphir reached the appointed spot, a scene of indescribable horror confronted them. News of their defeat had preceded them and mutilated corpses of some of the troops escorting Nadira, and articles of baggage were littered all over the place, with torn and blood-stained clothes, leather cases, jewellery boxes, tunics salwars, ghararas, female undergarments, slippers and toiletries. High in the sky, vultures were circling, while others were gorging themselves on the dead flesh and then were hopping about, finding it difficult to take off. There was no sign of the ladies or of the treasure. In one corner, Dara spied one of the guardsmen who had somehow managed to drag himself to a tree near the lip of the lake, against which he now lay propped up, with a gaping wound in his chest. Two vultures had settled themselves close to the man, waiting for him to breathe his last before they would tear off strips of flesh from him.

Dara dismounted and while an attendant accompanying him shooed the vultures away, he went up to the man, knelt down and held his ear close to the man's mouth. 'What happened?' he asked.

'Sire...when news of the defeat...' the man whispered, his lips barely moving as blood came frothing from his mouth, 'was received...some of the guards...' he paused to draw breath and then continued, his voice now even fainter than before, 'entrusted with the security of the ladies...attacked us. They stripped the ladies of their jewellery...and made off with them... They also took away the younger women and... the treasure...with them. Begum sahiba and Shahzadi sahiba managed to escape, Sire.'

'Which direction did they go?' asked Dara, now distraught with grief and concern.

With supreme effort, the man turned his head slightly in a south-westerly direction and then fell lifeless in Dara's arms.

'Come, Sire,' said an aide who was standing close by. 'We cannot lose a moment as the ladies continue to be in danger. From what this man indicates, most likely they have proceeded by the same route by which we advanced towards Ajmer.'

Dara nodded humbly. Maddened with anxiety as to the whereabouts of Nadira and Jahanzeb, he mounted wearily into the saddle and they rode forward in the direction in which the dying guardsman had pointed.

Meanwhile, Aurangzeb had been following the progress of the assault throughout the night and when news of the breach of Dara's elaborate fortifications through the successful attack from the rear reached his ears, he was elated.

'Excellent, Khan sahib,' he exclaimed, fixing Bahadur Khan, who stood before him with his piercing gaze. 'Your strategy has brought that infidel over to his knees. From this night onwards, you shall be ennobled as Khan-e-Dauran. Now don't let our brother get away. Pursue him to the ends of the earth if need be. Most likely he will try to scuttle back to Gujarat like a rat which seeks to find its hole. Let the word go forth from this time and place that anyone who gives succour and help to Dara will not only pay for it with his head, but he and all his descendants shall not live to see the next sunset.'

Late the following evening, Dara and Siphir caught sight of a small blur in the distance on the otherwise illimitable expanse of desert. Could it be Nadira and party? Hope welled up in Dara's heart and led by Multafat Khan, the party cautiously went forward. On coming closer, they found that indeed it was Nadira, Jahanzeb and the handful of guards who had stayed loyal to them, and in the confusion had whisked them away to safety when the others like ravening wolves were busy plundering and raping. The guards had now formed a protective circle around the ladies, but recognizing Dara they withdrew, allowing Dara and Nadira a few moments of privacy.

At seeing Dara, Nadira broke down. The iron self-control with which she had conducted herself all this while to give strength and courage to her husband forsook her. Great sobs wracked her body. Dara went up to her and drew her into his arms. As he held her head against his chest, her sobbing at length ceased.

'We were overwhelmed by the attack from the rear,' was all he could mumble in a broken voice, as if in explanation of his defeat.

Nadira nodded. Looking up at his drawn, haggard face, now bathed in sweat, with slack mouth and eyes bereft of all hope, she said nothing. What was there to say? The dice had been thrown one last time, and they had lost once again. Were they never to savour the fruits of victory? Were they forever to be harried and hounded by their implacable brother? What was left to them now but flight? Where would her husband take her now?

Maqbool came up to them. 'You may wish to rest for a short while, Sire,' he said gently. 'Prince Aurangzeb is bound to send troops in pursuit and we will have to set off very early tomorrow morning if we are to put a safe distance between them and us.'

As Nadira went to her carriage, Maqbool led Dara to a makeshift resting place screened by some torn and tattered panels, which had somehow been salvaged when the party fled from the camp near Ana Sagar, and which were now propped up by stakes dug into the ground. With a grateful glance at Maqbool, Dara shed the heavy breast plate that covered his torso and threw himself onto the rude bed made from straw cut for the horses and was covered with a rough under sheet. Gone were the concentric enclosures, rigorously patrolled by guards, the silken pavilions, the priceless carpets, the draperies, the golden ewers and the incense that marked the camp of the heir to the Mughal empire even when he was on the march. Now, all that separated him from those who had chosen to throw in their lot with him were these coarse panels through whose rents and tears, he could see the others in the camp bustling about in the firelight, while high above in the night sky, the stars could be seen wheeling majestically, supremely indifferent to the pitiful exertions of man below.

As Dara rested his head on a saddlebag and stretched his limbs, almost half-dead with fatigue, his mind was in turmoil. Was there still a chance that he would be able to retrieve his fortunes? But how? If he went back to Gujarat, would Shah Nawaz Khan help him raise another army? Would the aged governor risk Aurangzeb's wrath yet again to aid someone who had proved to be a consistent failure? If not Gujarat, then where? The Deccan? Kabul and then perhaps Persia? Would the Persian monarch extend the hand of friendship and aid in restoring Emperor Shah Jahan to his throne? After all, when the newly accredited Persian ambassador had presented his credentials the day the Emperor had fallen ill, which set in motion the whole litany of sorry events that had culminated in Dara's present condition, had not the ambassador referred to his master's pledges of eternal friendship and brotherhood? But would all those fine words uttered during the accreditation ceremony be translated into practice? Or, would they remain only words? Dara's mind harked back to that accreditation ceremony, and he was prepared to clutch at any straw. When was that? Less than two years ago? It seemed an eternity! How much water had flowed down the Jamuna since then leading to this sorry pass. As this welter of thoughts crowded Dara's mind, he fell into a fitful sleep.

Very early the next morning, Maqbool woke up Dara. 'Khan sahib advises that we move before dawn breaks, Sire. Enemy patrols are bound to be scouring the countryside and our only chance is to take advantage of the darkness and put as much distance as possible between them and us,' the faithful eunuch said, looking at his master with pity in his eyes, at the condition to which the Emperor's anointed heir had been brought.

Dara nodded. 'Which route does Khan sahib suggest we take?' he asked. Most of his generals had deserted him and having lost the powers of decision-making, he was now willing to be led by the captain of the guard.

'By the same route we advanced from Ahmedabad,' replied Maqbool . We have to reach Ahmedabad as soon as possible and seek Shah Nawaz Khan sahib's assistance to raise another army.'

As Dara got ready, Maqbool hurriedly woke the ladies up. What little baggage they had been able to retrieve while fleeing from Ana Sagar was hastily packed. The horses and camels were swiftly harnessed between the shafts of the carriages for the ladies, their girths were tightened and soon the party was on its way.

Meanwhile, remnants of Dara's army, which had fled in disorderly fashion after being overwhelmed at Deorai, were straggling along the same route that Dara was taking, and by the third night of their departure, about two thousand of them could be counted, some on horseback, others on foot— all strung along the dusty road but motivated more by the prospect of loot and plunder than any notions of loyalty to the heir apparent. Even so, their numbers were a welcome addition to Dara's pitiful numbers and were sufficient to overawe the small principalities through which the party rushed on their way to Ahmedabad. They remained unmolested as long as the force remained relatively close to each other, but woe betide those who fell back. Members of the Kuli tribe, who had made a profession out of robbery and brigandage and who moved in packs, were never very far away. They fell upon all those who got isolated or were too weak to resist. They were stripped of whatever valuables they had with them: swords, matchlocks, clothes, literally anything and then they were slashed to death and their naked, mutilated bodies left to rot by the wayside.

Jalore, Sirohi... As Dara passed along the outskirts of

these little towns, whose names tripped over his tongue, tired, despondent and woebegone, he recollected with what buoyant hopes he had crossed them only a few days earlier on the onward march towards Ajmer. How confident he had been that with Maharaja Jaswant Singh's assistance he would finally defeat his brother, erase all the humiliation he had suffered ever since the battle of Samugarh, rescue the Emperor from his confinement and in time ensure his own accession to the throne. Now all that was not to be and only a miracle could help him retrieve his fortunes.

Some days before they were to reach Ahmedabad late on evening, Multafat Khan slowed the pace of the carriages to a walk along the bank of a slender rivulet, as they had been travelling nearly all day non-stop and the horses were thoroughly exhausted. Nadira parted the curtains of her closed carriage and peered into the darkness. 'Where are we?' she asked.

Dara, who was a little behind, rode up. 'We are close to Deesa,' he said.

The memory of Deesa was particularly depressing for both Nadira and Dara, as it was while camping there that Nadira had initially voiced her reservations that Jaswant Singh might not march against Aurangzeb, since he had his own agenda to fulfil. And so it had come to pass. Bereft of Jaswant Singh's Rajputs, Dara's forces had been overwhelmed and now they were fleeing for their lives.

'Oh!' she said, looking into Dara's careworn face with defeat etched in his eyes.

'Don't worry,' he said, trying to sound cheerful. 'As soon as we reach Ahmedabad, I am confident things will brighten. Khan sahib I am sure will help us raise a fresh army and we shall return. This time, I have no doubt we will be victorious.'

'What did Abbu say?' asked Jahanzeb, who was also in the carriage, sleepily.

'He said that as soon as we reach Ahmedabad, we will equip a new army to do battle against your uncle and this time we will be successful.'

Jahanzeb sank back into her seat without saying a word.

Nadira drew the curtain. Both she and Jahanzeb knew that what Dara was saying was only to keep up their spirits, but his voice betrayed his emotions. It was apparent that he himself did not have much faith in his words. *What was there to say in reply?* thought Nadira to herself. What use would recriminations be? They seemed destined to spend the rest of their lives driven from place to place, hunted and harried by their ruthless and implacable brother till merciful death put an end to their suffering.

As the party proceeded further through the desert, Nadira had half a mind to tell Dara to give up all claims to the throne and surrender himself to Aurangzeb's mercy seeking only that he be allowed to retire in peace and dwell quietly with his family in some distant part of the empire, far from the haunts of man. Surely, Aurangzeb would not grudge them a little spot of earth, where they could build a roof over their heads and she would see her children grow up in peace and tranquillity. Yes, it would be a great downfall from being the mistress of a great empire, but would Dara ever have the chance of ruling it? She knew her husband well enough to realize that he stood no chance against his ruthless, determined brother and now with Jaswant Singh's Rajputs too turning away, and the debacle at Deorai, perhaps the last chance of retrieving the empire had been lost.

As the party approached Ahmedabad, two outriders were sent out at the gallop to inform Shah Nawaz Khan of the party's arrival and their return was eagerly awaited. Meanwhile, signs of habitation began to appear and the scenery became progressively greener. They passed villages surrounded by small fields brimming—some with water, the odd palm tree studding the landscape and people going about performing the immemorial tasks of rural life.

Late one evening, the party found itself on a slight eminence, from where a little smudge on the horizon could be discerned. They were the fortress walls of Ahmedabad. A cheer went up among the assembled group and a smile broke on Dara's careworn face. Ahmedabad! At last! Now help would be at hand. They could rest after the arduous journey; the treasure could be recouped and a fresh army fitted out to battle the usurper. A vista of possibilities opened out. Soon, Shah Nawaz Khan, with his retinue of nobles, would ride out to receive them and they would be escorted with due pomp and ceremony though the fortress gates. As the party tried to spruce itself up in what was actually a pitiful recreation of the splendour of their outward journey, one of the outriders could be seen riding furiously towards them, weaving through the undergrowth, while the other one was nowhere to be seen. When the rider approached the party, his path was blocked by one of the guards standing some distance away from Dara, but the rider dismounted, brushed aside the guard and threw himself at Dara's feet.

'The…gates…of the…fort…are closed, Your Highness,' he managed to blurt out before collapsing to the ground. From the back of his head, below his helmet, blood was seeping out, staining the ground.

'Quick, call hakeem sahib,' Dara cried. 'Meanwhile, get some water.'

Dara was dumbstruck. What had happened? Why were the gates closed? Who had assaulted the outriders? Had anything happened to Shah Nawaz Khan? Would it be a repetition of what had occurred outside the walls of Delhi? These thoughts kept churning in Dara's mind as he waited for the outrider to draw breath.

As Dara's servants ran to obey his bidding, he knelt down and cradled the man's head in his arms, trying as best as he could to staunch the blood. When the water was brought, he wet his handkerchief and wiped the man's face with it and then held it against his wound. Just then the hakeem arrived with some bandages and a salve, which he applied on the wound. Gradually, the outrider's eyes fluttered open.

'When we reached the fort, we found the gates closed,' he said, putting in all his effort. 'Through the embrasures in the battlements we could see the barrels of cannons and muskets, and a large body of men were manning the walls as if they were ready to repel an attack. On reaching the gate, we shouted that we have come in peace and that we were members from Prince Dara's party, upon which they opened fire at us. We turned to get away as fast as we could, but a bullet caught Mustaq in the back and he fell from his horse. Another bullet grazed my neck, Sire, but I was able to make good my escape.'

'It is not safe to go anywhere near the fort, Your Highness,' said Multafat Khan. 'See what they have done to our messenger. It seems that Nawab sahib is no longer in command of the fort. Let me go and find out what the actual position is.'

Multafat Khan signalled to the others to stay back and spurred his horse forward. Dara drew rein and nodded forlornly.

Just then Multafat Khan saw a mounted courier approaching the fort from behind them and advancing towards the fort. The fact that he was undeterred by the bristling guns on the ramparts gave reason for Multafat Khan to believe that the courier was aware of the present position inside the fort.

'Why is the gate not being opened? Multafat Khan asked him when he drew near. 'Are the lookouts posted in the tower not aware that Prince Dara and his party are awaiting entrance?'

'Do you not know? Shah Nawaz Khan has been arrested. Mudassar Gul is now in charge of the fort and he has strict orders from Prince Aurangzeb himself not to let anyone in without orders,' the courier replied, nodding towards Dara and the rest of the party which waited in the distance. The man sounded triumphant.

Mudassar Gul, the naib governor of the fort, had very early on indicated his adherence to the rising sun, and had tried to persuade Shah Nawaz to do so even while Dara was in Ahmedabad, so much so that he had to be placed under house arrest. It was clear that during Dara's march northwards, Gul had succeeded in winning over a sufficient number of adherents to his cause to seize the fort and detain Shah Nawaz Khan.

When Multafat Khan carried the news to Dara, he was beside himself with grief and concern—not so much for himself now, for he was fast reaching a stage where he was past caring what would happen to himself, but how he was to break the news to Nadira. For the last few days, her spells of coughing had increased and she had begun to suffer from dysentery. How would she take the news?

When Nadira saw Dara approaching her with his drawn face, she instinctively realized that he brought bad tidings.

'Nawab sahib has been arrested,' he said shortly. 'Mudassar Gul is now in charge. He has received strict orders from Aurangzeb himself not to open the gates for us.'

'Ya Allah,' Nadira cried as she fell into a deep faint.

Nine

The night was dark. A thin sickle moon hung in the sky among a scattering of stars over Dara's pitifully small camp, which was now reduced to a few dozen troopers and aides amidst the boulders and scree of the Balochistan hills. Dara's own tent stood a little distance away from the others to give its occupants a measure of privacy, but the gaping rents in the tent's panels, which were fastened crudely to the overhanging boughs of trees that stood close by, had their own sad story to tell. Once again, the party had crossed the trackless wastes of the Rann of Kutch, and negotiated the barren emptiness of eastern Sindh, fleeing westwards as they were pursued by troops under the overall command of Mirza Raja Jai Singh, who had been deputed by Aurangzeb to capture Dara. With each passing day, Nadira had grown progressively weaker and she was increasingly coughing blood, which greatly hampered their speed, but Dara was anxious to put as much distance as possible between his party and his pursuers. He felt they would be safer once they reached the Indus River.

❦

'The prince is within our grasp, Your Highness,' Rao Raja Madho Singh, who was one of Jai Singh's most intrepid captains, had said midway during the chase when he had gone up to Jai Singh one night, who was sitting outside his pavilion, sipping his fiery drink of aasa. 'Prince Dara's forces are deserting him in droves, as they are convinced that his cause is now hopeless and those who have surrendered today say that the number of active combatants is less than a hundred. The rest are the usual hangers-on, who have nowhere to go and in any case would be useless in battle. Even his trusted lieutenant Nawab Dawood Khan is no longer with him. It is said that hot words were exchanged between the two when the Nawab advised Prince Dara that there was still time to make an elaborate feint and then to proceed towards the Deccan, and therefore he should make common cause with the Marathas and the other southern kingdoms. It was a proposition that Prince Dara angrily rejected, placing greater faith in support from the Persians. It is rumoured that Prince Dara intends to cross the Indus River at Sehwan, head for the Bolan Pass and then flee into Afghanistan. Let me take a hundred sowars, Your Highness, and I assure you that I will bring Prince Dara in chains within a week. Once he crosses the Indus, our task will become much more difficult.'

Jai Singh had looked into the expectant eyes of his young captain, glinting in the firelight, who seemed to be straining at the leash to capture Dara. What could be a greater prize for Madho Singh than to bring the prince imperial, on whose head an enormous bounty had been placed, in chains? Jai Singh, too, could then bask in the reflected glory. Yet, Jai Singh had hesitated. He had a lingering respect for the one who after all was still the rightful heir to the Mughal throne, and realizing that Dara would risk facing death in hand-to-hand combat to avoid capture, he did not want the blood of the Emperor's son on his hands. He felt it would be sufficient if Dara was expelled beyond the frontiers of the empire. Explanations could be offered to Aurangzeb later.

'Hmm, I shall let you know my decision in due course,' he had replied, but he took care to ensure that at least one day's march intervened between his frontline troops and Dara's party, allowing the fugitive prince to cross the Indus and traverse the pitiless desert of Sindh into Balochistan without being intercepted.

༺ঞ্জ৽

Now by the flickering light of an oil lamp that stood in the corner of the tent, Nadira could be seen lying motionless upon the narrow pallet that was her bed, except when she drew breath in great gasps, while Siphir and Jahanzeb dozed fitfully in one corner and Dara kept mopping her fevered brow with a damp handkerchief.

Suddenly, a great paroxysm of coughing overtook Nadira. She sat up clutching her throat as her body shook spasmodically and gobbets of sputum streaked with blood dribbled down her mouth, which Dara wiped away before she lay back again. By this time, the hakeems accompanying Dara's party had fled, taking with them all their pills and powders, and leaving behind only the leeches, which having gorged all day on Nadira's blood, now lay in their dish twitching torpidly.

Dara was beside himself with concern. What was he to do now? Siphir and Jahanzeb, who had woken up, rushed to their mother's bedside. Dara tenderly propped her up in a sitting position and signalled to Maqbool, who had by this time entered the tent, to pour some water in a cup, which he held to Nadira's lips. She had barely taken a sip when her body was again convulsed in an acute spasm of coughing, with more blood spewing out of her mouth this time. It was clear that the end was not far-off. With a superhuman effort, she reached out her hands to grasp those of Siphir and Jahanzab, who were kneeling on either side of her bed.

Looking at Dara with pain-filled eyes, and with her lips barely moving, she muttered, 'Look after them,' and then fell back, eyes closed. Dara and Maqbool tried vigorously to massage the soles of her feet, hoping to revive her, but it was to no avail. A little while later, Nadira breathed her last.

A great groan of grief escaped Dara's lips as he beheld the lifeless body of his dearly beloved wife, who had been through so much suffering and had stood by him all these years. Tears welled in his eyes, and he drew Siphir and Jahanzeb close to his chest. Had he brought nothing except trouble and tribulation to his family? Would there be no end to it?

As one by one the stars disappeared and dawn broke, preparations were made for Nadira's final journey. During one of their conversations, Nadira had said that she would like to be interred close to the tomb of Dara's own preceptor Mian Mir in Lahore and Dara was determined to fulfil her wish. A rough coffin was fashioned out of the trees growing nearby and the body was laid reverently in it, which was then packed with grass and straw to withstand the long journey. The Fateha was intoned by a qazi who had miraculously stayed behind. The few troopers who still remained with Dara were detailed to escort the body of the Mughal princess to Lahore. As he saw the funeral cortège dwindling to become a mere speck in the distance, Dara was left with his two children, the faithful Maqbool, a few of Nadira's handmaidens and some servants.

Consumed with grief, Dara remained in a stupor for two whole days. None dared intrude upon the wall of silence he had built around himself, but on the third day, he roused himself and took stock of his situation. A day's march west from his camp and not far from the Bolan Pass stood Dadar, the hill fort of Jiwan Malik, an Afghan chieftain who owed his life to Dara for having saved him from Shah Jahan's wrath when he had failed to send troops to defend Kandahar against the Persians six years earlier. Surely, reasoned Dara, the debt that Malik owed him combined with the traditions of Afghan hospitality would ensure that he would not be turned away from the chieftain's door. With a little help from the Afghan, he could cross the Bolan Pass and reach Kandahar, from where he could proceed to Kabul and once again throw the dice for the Mughal throne.

'Do not trust him, Sire,' warned Maqbool, when he heard of Dara's plan to seek Malik's help to cross the Bolan Pass. 'His reputation in these parts is such that it is said that he would sell his own mother if it was advantageous for himself. I have this in confidence from practically all the villagers whose habitations we have passed in this godforsaken region.'

'He owes his life to me,' replied Dara. 'Surely that should count for something. Had it not been for me, his corpse would have been hanging from a gibbet, so furious was the Emperor at his dereliction of duty during the siege of Kandahar.'

Maqbool noticed that Dara had used the humbler 'me' to the royal 'us'.

How had the mighty fallen!

'Moreover, what alternative do we have?' Dara continued. 'Having come this far, we can only proceed ahead. All we shall ask from Malik are a few horses and a small escort to enable us to reach Kandahar. From there, we will make our way to Kabul, where I am sure to find support. Malik knows that he will be highly recompensed once the Emperor is seated back upon the throne. I shall personally see to that.'

Maqbool kept his peace but looked with sadness not unmixed with pity at his master. Here was Dara hanging on by his eyelids at the very outer fringes of the empire, with no troops, no guns and with nothing except a few women, eunuchs and servants, placing his trust in a rogue chieftain to wrest the throne of Delhi from his implacable brother. Had he learnt nothing at all? After all that he has been through?

∽∾∾

'Welcome to the humble abode of your servant, Your Highness,' said Jiwan Malik as he rode out and greeted Dara effusively, some distance from the gates of his fort after dismounting, while Dara and his party wended their way towards it. Malik was a tall, heavily built man with beady eyes and the scar of a sword slash running down the right side of his face, which his beard failed to conceal. His spies had been reporting Dara's every move since the party had entered his territory and lookouts atop the fort gates had been regularly reporting to him as the party negotiated the winding, stony pathway to the fort.

'We met last under more pleasant circumstances,' murmured Dara, smiling weakly and assuming as much authority as he could muster, as if to remind Jiwan Malik that it was in his presence and at his intercession that the Emperor had pardoned the Afghan with his life.

'To be sure, to be sure, Your Highness,' exclaimed Jiwan Malik heartily as he led the party to the fort, not omitting a single act of etiquette and courtesy. 'How can it be forgotten that but for your benign intercession, this humble creature would have been shortened by a head.'

On reaching the fort, Malik said, 'Your Highness and the party must be tired. Please treat this fort as your own and rest here as long as you wish to. Meanwhile, please let me know your future plans and if I can be of any use in their furtherance, Your Highness has only to command.'

For three days and three nights, Dara and his party enjoyed Jiwan Malik's hospitality, who spared nothing to minister to Dara's comforts and to make him and his party feel at home. They sat on the same carpet and ate from the same dastarkhwan. At last Dara felt relieved. Jiwan Malik was indeed redeeming the debt he owed to Dara. How wrong Maqbool had been to doubt the Afghan's sincerity!

On the morning of the fourth day, Dara was ready to depart from Malik's fort for the onward journey to the Bolan Pass. He had sought for an armed escort of fifty men to accompany him up to the pass and beyond, which Malik had promised to furnish. Malik and a few of his aides accompanied him for some distance down the road, but not sighting the escort party anywhere in the vicinity, Dara asked, 'We do not see the escort you had promised us, Sardar sahib. Where are they?'

At that instant, upon a signal given by Malik, a group of heavily armed horsemen emerged from behind a clump of trees.

'Here they are, Your Highness,' roared Malik.

Before Dara could realize what was happening, the party had been surrounded, and the servants and eunuchs separated from the women and swiftly trussed up with the ropes which the men had brought along with them. Now that Dara and his party were not under Malik's roof, the Afghan was no longer bound by the traditions of hospitality of his race.

Dara saw Siphir trying to reach for his sword and instinctively he dug his heels into the flanks of his horse to rush to the boy's assistance, but he was too late. A gigantic Afghan trooper bore down upon Siphir with levelled lance and held its point within an inch of his throat, ready to skewer him if he made so much as a false move. He looked at Dara menacingly.

Seeing that his son was in mortal danger if he advanced any further, Dara backed away, fast realizing that his party was heavily outnumbered, without arms and burdened by women, and any resistance would be useless. Reining his horse and swivelling in his saddle to face Malik, he cried in impotent rage. 'You blackguard, you treacherous, misbegotten scoundrel! Is this the gratitude you show to me for having saved your life, when the Emperor wanted to flay you alive? Ya Allah, what evil stars made me put my trust in a faithless rogue such as you, who betrayed my father and now has betrayed me in this hour of need.'

Hearing this, one of the troopers was about to pull Dara down from his horse and strike him across the face, but a stern look from the Afghan chieftain and he sheepishly lowered his hand. Jiwan Malik's only interest was to deliver Dara and his family in one piece to Aurangzeb and claim his reward, which he knew would be stupendous. Meanwhile, let the prince bluster and fulminate as much as he wanted to. Words never hurt anybody.

Malik did not as much as glance at Dara as the cavalcade rode back to the fort. On reaching its gates, he turned to his trusted aide Abdul Ghafoor. 'Ensure that the Shahzadeh and the children are properly guarded at all times, but see that no harm comes to them. Send a fast rider to inform

Mirza Raja Jai Singh and Bahadur Khan, who are by now perhaps returning to Delhi, that Prince Dara and his children are in my custody and I shall personally hand them over at any place and date along the way that they may choose. As for the women and the menials, distribute them among the soldiery.'

As Ghafoor nodded and went forward to carry out his master's bidding, Jiwan Malik turned on his heel and proceeded towards his private apartments.

Ten

'**B**ahadur Khan and Jiwan Malik have arrived with the captives, Sire. They beg audience with Your Majesty,' an aide announced as Aurangzeb was conferring with Taufiq Hasan, his chief confidential agent in the Diwan-e-Khas of the Red Fort in Delhi.

'Yes, show them in,' replied Aurangzeb, a smirk on his face. 'We look forward to hearing how our brother has fared in the course of his travels, which has finally brought him to our doorstep.'

Aurangzeb had been getting daily reports of the progress of the party as it proceeded towards Delhi and now finally his hated brother was firmly within his grasp.

The aide bowed and withdrew.

A little while later, the two were ushered in. Aurangzeb threw a questioning glance at them. 'So you are the one who finally ran our brother down to earth,' he said, fixing Jiwan Malik with a glittering eye.

The Afghan nodded, bursting with pride.

'You have risen in our esteem and shall be suitably rewarded.' Then turning to Bahadur Khan, he added, 'But the slow pace of your advance disappointed us. According to reports that we were receiving regularly, a little more celerity on the part of the imperial forces, and our brother and his entire party could have been intercepted well before they crossed the Indus River. How do you explain the delay?'

'Mirza sahib was in overall command of the expedition, Sire,' replied Bahadur Khan as he squirmed under Aurangzeb's unrelenting gaze and tried as best as he could to defend himself. 'In fact, I tried several times to persuade him to send flying columns to intercept the fugitives before they crossed the Indus, and some of his own captains tried to do so too, but he seemed reluctant to do so, although I cannot fathom the reason for this reluctance.'

'Perhaps we can,' replied Aurangzeb. 'Perhaps he thought he had discharged his duties by driving that infidel beyond the frontiers of the empire when our specific instructions were that he should be brought bound hand and foot before us. Worse, perhaps he feels that our brother has still a chance of ascending the throne and did not want to sunder links completely with him. We shall call him to account when he next appears in court,' with a curt nod Aurangzeb dismissed Bahadur Khan and Jiwan Malik.

'We propose to put this mendacious infidel before a court of qazis to pronounce on his fate,' continued Aurangzeb, turning back to Hasan. 'Let it never be said that our decisions were not guided by the tenets of sharia law. Meanwhile, we intend to make a spectacle of him. It is time that the people of Delhi got to know the fate of those who stand against the empire.'

A few mornings later, by beat of drum, the people of Delhi were summoned out onto the streets to witness a sight they would remember for the rest of their lives. As the sun rose, the Lahori Gate of the capital city opened and seated in an open howdah, chained and clad in rags atop a small, dirty female elephant, with a filthy turban on his head, was Dara, the very picture of despair and humiliation, with Siphir by his side. A gigantic trooper sat behind them with drawn sword, ready to decapitate them at any attempt to escape, while cavalrymen and mounted archers, led by Bahadur Khan, formed an iron cordon round the royal prisoner. Wending their way through the principal streets of Delhi, the grim procession went up the stately Chandni Chowk, while the huge crowd of people who had thronged the route, at places three or four deep, rent the air with their piercing wails and shrieks, beating their chests with their fists, lamenting the fate of the heir to the Mughal empire, whom an unjust fate had reduced to such circumstances.

'What malevolent destiny has brought our Prince to this sorry pass,' cried a wizened old man, throwing up his arms in the air as the troopers surrounding Dara and Siphir passed him. 'He's a good person, who has always tried to bind people of different faiths together. Why is this being done to him?'

'Man's fate is inscribed on his forehead,' intoned another as he peered with rheumy eyes at the cavalcade. 'It is only Allah who can erase or obliterate what is written.'

'Oh look at Prince Siphir!' said a woman, peering through the eye slits of her burka. 'Surely he does not deserve such a fate.'

Through it all, Dara sat in the howdah with a drawn face, looking straight ahead, trying to muster up as much courage and dignity as he could. Now and then, he leaned over a little to whisper words of encouragement to Siphir. As dusk drew near, the melancholy cavalcade having traversed most of the main thoroughfares and narrower alleys of Delhi finally wended its way to the dungeons of Khizrabad, where Dara and Siphir were incarcerated.

Taufiq Hasan had stationed his agents in disguise along the entire route, who had been sending him regular reports on the people's reaction to Dara being thus paraded. Late that evening, he sought audience with the monarch.

'The people of Delhi were highly distressed with what they saw during the day, Sire,' began Hasan as Aurangzeb heard his chief agent out in silence. 'Cries of lamentation could be heard along the entire route from Hindus and Muslims alike. Some of the Afghan troopers who were out making purchases in one of the alleys were attacked by a mob. Filth and refuse were hurled at them from the gutter, and they had a hard time extricating themselves from the fury of the populace. Indeed, Sire, you will pardon this unworthy creature for saying so, but whatever decision Your Majesty may have in store for Prince Dara, my only submission is that it may be taken quickly, well before the situation gets out of hand.'

Aurangzeb saw the wisdom in Taufiq Hasan's advice. He knew that his hold over the empire was not yet secure and he was shrewd enough to realize that several Rajput nobles would prefer to see Dara, with his tolerant, ecumenical attitude towards Hinduism, seated upon the throne rather than himself. Moreover, disaffected members of the Muslim nobility whom Aurangzeb had not been able to gratify with the grant of large estates and high offices of state could make common cause with them, and finding support from Emperor Shah Jahan, who was still alive, attempts could even be made to set Dara free and project him as the rightful heir to the throne. The last thing Aurangzeb wanted on his hands was trouble in the capital city of the empire.

'We have already made our intention known of bringing our brother before a court of qazis to pronounce their verdict on his various acts of omission and commission. There is no point in delaying that,' Aurangzeb murmured as he clapped his hands to summon a servitor.

'Ask Maulvi Muhammed Ibrahim Sarhadi, Shamshul Faraz and Mir Mustaq to meet us forthwith,' Aurangzeb ordered.

The attendant bowed and withdrew to carry out the order.

In short order, the three leading clerics in Delhi presented themselves before Aurangzeb.

'You are aware that our brother has never acknowledged his unswerving allegiance to the true faith, and ever since he grew to manhood has spent time and treasure in the fruitless pursuit of finding commonalities between Islam and other religions,' began Aurangzeb, fixing the three men who stood before him with a stern eye. 'Indeed, we view this as the height of apostasy, and it is fit that he answer for it before any further attempts are made by him to corrupt the minds of the gullible, which could shake the very foundations of the empire. As we are guided by the tenets of sharia law in all our actions, we propose to put him on trial and call upon you as its most learned interpreters to judge him and pronounce your verdict without delay.'

The qazis were dismissed with a curt nod. As they retreated with deep salaams, a quiet smile of triumph broke upon Aurangzeb's lips. He knew that the three clerics were extremely conservative in their outlook, and Dara's fate would be effectively sealed.

News that Dara would be tried by a court of qazis spread rapidly, and two mornings later, the chamber of the Diwan-e-Khas, where Dara was to be tried, was thronged with noblemen, well before the proceedings were to commence. With considerable gravity, the three qazis filed in and took their seats on a raised masnad as Aurangzeb watched from behind the screen of the raised gallery that ran around the chamber, from where the ladies of the court usually watched the court proceedings below.

'Let the prisoner be brought forth,' said Maulvi Sarhadi, the senior most of the three, in a loud voice, who sat between the other two. He was a corpulent man of middle height, with beady eyes, a fleshy nose and a straggly beard.

The hum of conversation ceased and a hush descended on the chamber as Dara was led in, escorted by two soldiers, one on either side, his hands manacled and his feet bound in golden fetters. Sarhadi made a motion towards the carpet that lay spread out before him as Dara, with some difficulty, sat down upon it. Just as the trial was about to begin, high up in the gallery, there was a rustle of silk as Roshanara Begum, along with some of her ladies-in-waiting, entered the gallery and sat down gracefully by Aurangzeb's side with folded knees on the cushions that were strewn on the marble floor.

Aurangzeb and Roshanara exchanged glances.

'Muhammad Dara Shukoh, you are here before us this morning to answer to the high crime of deliberately attempting to drag down the true faith from its exalted pedestal by seeking to find common ground between it and other religions. Do you plead guilty or not guilty?' began Sarhadi.

'Before I answer—'

'Do you plead guilty or not guilty?' thundered Sarhadi harshly.

'Not guilty,' replied Dara in a low voice.

'Is it not true that under your directions, texts from some

of the Hindu holy books such as the Upanishads and the Bhagavad Gita were ordered to be translated into Farsi?' asked Sarhadi.

'Not only the books of the Hindus. The holy book of those who profess the Christian faith too,' piped in Mir Mustaq in his thin, reedy voice.

'I do not deny it,' replied Dara.

'What was your objective?' asked Shamshul Faraz.

'Since childhood, I have been interested in the study of comparative religions, worthy clerics. My conversations with Hindu scholars have led me to believe that there are certain truths embedded in their religion, and likewise certain Christian divines have sought to convince me that the path to salvation lay in their religion. However, there are wide divergences in the interpretations given by seers and priests belonging to these religions at different points in time. My objective in commissioning these translations was to go to the original sources to test some of these claims against the touchstone of the eternal teachings of Islam to see how far these claims were correct. These studies were undertaken by me only for my own benefit, in my own private capacity, and were not to travel beyond the four walls of the palace,' replied Dara.

'What benefit did you seek to derive from them? Have you any doubts that the word of God as revealed to Prophet Muhammad, may peace be upon him, and contained in the Holy Koran represents the ultimate truth, and there is no need to burrow into the texts of other religions? Or, is it that you doubt that the Holy Koran contains the full and complete truth?' chimed in Sarhadi.

'Not at all, worthy clerics. Indeed, far from it. To my

understanding, Islam is a perfect religion and caters to all human needs in this world and the hereafter. However, Sufi mysticism, which has contributed so much to the spread of the true faith, and the Bhakti movement in Hinduism, which is gaining wide acceptance among the people, share certain similarities. Both seek to pierce the veil of illusion to shed light on the reality that lies behind it, and both emphasize man's oneness with God, though they differ on the means to achieve it. It is such elements of congruence and divergence that I have been seeking to explore.'

'Do you think that consorting with Hindu scholars and Christian divines in night-long sessions, and sponsoring such studies behoves a person of your station in life and could remain hidden from the people and not get talked about in every nook and corner of the empire, with grave consequences to its peace and stability?' asked Shamshul Faraz.

Dara remained silent.

'Is it also not a fact that you had commissioned a translation of the Hindu epic Ramayana into Farsi?' asked Shamshul Faraz.

'That is true,' replied Dara in a low voice.

'Are you not thereby seeking congruence in the text of a Hindu epic with the word of God as revealed in the Holy Koran?' asked Shamshul Faraz.

'Ram is worshipped as a god by the Hindus, worthy clerics and my studies reveal to me that God is one, although he is called by different names—'

'Howsoever Ram is worshipped by Hindus, do you deny that the Ramayana is the work of mortal man?' interjected Maulvi Sarhadi. 'Think well before you answer. Remember, we, too, are not unfamiliar with the Hindu epics.'

'I am aware of its provenance,' replied Dara.

'And do you deny that the Holy Koran is the word of God revealed to the Prophet, may peace be upon him?' asked Sarhadi.

'How can I deny that which is the truth—'

'And yet you seek congruence in the two?' interjected Maulvi Sarhadi, looking at the other two clerics, who sat on either side of him, with a self-satisfied smile on his face as if he had scored a major debating point.

'Do you deny that this book *Majma'al-Bahrayan* was written by you?' Shamshul Faraz picked up a beautifully bound volume with gold lettering in exquisite Persian Nastaliq calligraphy that lay by his side with obvious distaste, using only two fingers of his hand and waved it aloft in the air.

'I do not deny it,' mumbled Dara.

'Hmm... The title means the "Meeting Place of Two Oceans". Which are the two oceans that you refer to? asked Mir Mustaq in a deceptively innocent voice. He had been silent during a large part of the exchange.

'Islam and Hinduism,' replied Dara.

'Is that not sufficient proof that you seek to find affinities in the two religions?' asked Mir Mustaq.

Dara remained silent.

'To what end? Answer us,' barked Sarhadi harshly.

'To help me achieve a better understanding of some of the basic truths of Islam, the faith I hold above all others,' replied Dara.

'Lies. Utter lies,' shouted Sarhadi. 'You want us to believe that not being satisfied with the interpretations given by some of the most learned Islamic scholars on the Holy Koran, you have been scouring the texts of other religions to better understand your own? In the translations of the Upanishads that you commissioned, titled *Sirre-Akbar* or The Greatest Mystery, the suggestion has been advanced that the *Kitab-e-Maknoun* mentioned in the Holy Koran is also referred to in the Upanishads?'

At the mention of this juxtaposition, there was general hubbub in the Diwan-e-Khas as the assembled courtiers and noblemen looked at each other in astonishment.

Sarhadi held his hand up to ensure silence. Up in the gallery, behind the screen, Aurangzeb and Roshanara had been watching the proceedings intently.

'Let us see how our brother will wriggle out of that,' murmured Roshanara to Aurangzeb through thin lips set in a hard face.

'I had no intention of showing any disrespect to the true faith, learned clerics. It was only a tentative suggestion that this line of questioning should be explored further,' was all that Dara could mumble.

'Enough. Let the prisoner be led away. We shall now retire to deliberate on our verdict,' Sarhadi said as he and the other two qazis rose from the masnad and proceeded to a small antechamber that abutted the Diwan-e-Khas.

Half a watch later, the three qazis presented themselves before Aurangzeb, who was closeted with his close counsellors. By that time, the other courtiers had drifted away.

'Well, have you reached a verdict?' Aurangzeb asked.

'We have, Your Majesty,' replied Sarhadi.

'What is it?'

'Guilty, Your Majesty, for violating the holy tenets of Islam by lowering the true faith from its high pedestal in seeking to find commonalities between it and other religions, with profoundly adverse consequences on the peace and stability of the empire,' replied Sarhadi gravely.

'Is the verdict unanimous?' asked Aurangzeb.

Sarhadi looked at the other two qazis standing on either side of him and then nodded his assent.

'And the penalty for such a grave crime?'

'We leave that to you, Your Majesty, but may I submit that capital punishment has been inflicted on persons for far lesser offences.'

'You have done well to have pronounced your verdict clearly and without circumlocution,' said Aurangzeb as the qazis bowed and withdrew.

Then turning to his counsellors and raising a quizzical eyebrow, Aurangzeb said, 'You heard the qazis. How do we proceed now?'

Those present had read Aurangzeb's mind and knew exactly the reply he wanted. Yet, each was unwilling to speak first and kept looking at each other, waiting for someone else to begin. Finally, Iqbal Mohammed Khan broke the silence. 'As long as Prince Dara lives, Your Highness, he will a source of disquiet in the empire. The Marathas are still not subdued, Bengal is in ferment and many of the Rajput princes are sitting on the fence. In fact, the affection and sympathy that the people of Delhi displayed towards him the other day, when he was taken out on elephant back, is not hidden from anyone. You will pardon me for speaking frankly, Sire, but even factions within the nobility, whom I need not name, could use his presence to stir unrest, claiming that as Emperor Shah Jahan's eldest son, by the law of primogeniture, he has a superior claim to the throne.'

'When did the law of primogeniture ever govern succession

in the house of Timur?' remarked Aurangzeb with a short, cynical laugh. 'With us, it has always been the takht. However, do continue.'

'As I was submitting, Your Highness, now that we have the highest religious and judicial opinion to draw upon, no blame will attach if Prince Dara is eased from the burdens of life.'

Aurangzeb threw a glance at Shaista Khan, one of the grandees of the empire, who had thrown in his lot with the present regime on the promise of wide estates in Awadh. 'I am in agreement with Khan sahib,' he said shortly.

Aurangzeb then turned to Danishmand Khan, the court chamberlain, who he knew was not afraid to air a contrarian view. Indeed, like many shrewd rulers, Aurangzeb did not like to be surrounded only by yes-men. Clearing his throat and mustering his courage, Danishmand began, 'While much that has been said carries weight, my own view is that no useful purpose will be served by extinguishing Prince Dara's life, at least at this stage. Indeed, when the history of Your Majesty's reign is written, it will always be considered a black mark that will disfigure its start in the absence of any overt act that would justify his execution. Let him live, Your Majesty, immersed in his books and his fantasies for the present at any rate, and let it be seen by the whole world that the empire is ruled by one who tempers firmness with mercy. No doubt, the prince should remain in close custody for the rest of his natural life and if any attempt is made to use him to cause unrest, well then, a decision to end his life can be taken, but at this stage, in my humble opinion, sufficient cause has not been shown to put him to death.'

'We thank you for your advice on this momentous issue,' said Aurangzeb, sweeping the three with his steely eyes. 'Rest assured it will receive our earnest consideration.'

As Aurangzeb grappled with the decision on the future course of action to be adopted, later that day, Roshanara sought audience with him. 'I was informed that you were in conference with your counsellors to decide on the fate of our brother. Has a decision been taken?'

'No, not yet,' replied Aurangzeb.

'Put him out of the way. Let not the start of your reign be disfigured by an infidel such as him, whose very shadow is a curse. A just fate has made you the ruler of a great empire, which can truly become a Dar al-Islam a home for the true believers, if apostasy such as the one practised by our brother is mercilessly crushed. As long as he lives, his pernicious views will find shelter in some corner of the empire, with scope for mischief and unforeseen consequences. Indeed, trying to trace the *Kitab-e-Maknoun* in the Holy Koran to the Upanishads is the last straw and makes his offence all the more culpable. Let the world be rid of those who harbour such impious thoughts.' With these words ringing in Aurangzeb's ears, Roshanara swept out of the room.

Any lingering doubts or hesitation that Aurangzeb might have had on his future course of action regarding Dara were dissipated after hearing what Roshanara had said. Yes, Dara had to be put to death for the preservation of his own hold on the throne if not for any other reason. Moreover, had he not forsaken the life of a fakir to commune with God and come back into the world in order to rule them to make the empire a true home for all believers? As long as Dara lived, that pious objective would always be in jeopardy, and dangerous, free thinking ideas such as his, espoused by one who happened to be the Emperor's eldest son, concealed within their fold the scope for unending mischief, even if he were in captivity. It was best that the life of this enemy of the true faith was forfeited in the larger imperial interest, while the unanimous verdict of the highest ecclesiastical court in the realm was still fresh in the public mind.

∽

Meanwhile, back in his cell, Dara paced the floor restlessly, his hopes dwindling with each passing hour, as Siphir sat in a corner on the earthen floor, looking disconsolately at the last shred of light visible through the grill set high in the wall.

'Father, they will release us, won't they? he asked at length plaintively.

'Any time now, my son. Have courage. Our troubles will soon be over and we will be set free.' Even as Dara said that, inwardly he was filled with trepidation. What would be the decision? Would they at least allow him to live? From the questions put to him by the qazis he was aware that he could expect no reprieve, but the final decision lay with Aurangzeb. Dara knew that before taking any decision, Aurangzeb would sound out his closest advisers. What advice would Iqbal Mohammed Khan and Shaista Khan give? Of them, Dara was aware that both would tailor their advice to suit exactly what Aurangzeb wanted, but Danishmand Khan? Ah, there was some hope there, but would his brother listen to that advice? What about Roshanara? He knew that there was little love lost between him and her, but would she advise the death of her own brother? Now that all of Dara's ambitions had been finally crushed by the remorseless turn of fate, and he was at Aurangzeb's absolute mercy, would not his younger brother and sister at least allow him to live? After all, what did he ask for? A roof over his head, some food, his beloved books, some paper, ink and quills. He would be no threat to anyone, and would be happy to spend the rest of his life in total obscurity.

All these thoughts coursed through Dara's mind and as no news of his fate reached him, he grew increasingly desperate. Perhaps, if he threw himself at Aurangzeb's feet, there was some glimmer of hope. Calling for some paper and ink from the guard who was moved to pity at the plight of the royal prisoner, Dara, with a shaky hand, scribbled these lines.

My Lord Brother,

All thoughts of challenging your authority have been abandoned by me and all I now seek is your mercy. I place my head under your feet and humbly seek your pardon for my transgressions. In the name of Allah, the Compassionate and Merciful, I beseech to allow me to live with the bare essentials far away in some forgotten corner of the empire, causing trouble to none. A place where I shall pass the remaining days of my life in contemplation of Allah, praying for your success and good fortune.

When Aurangzeb received this missive, his eyes gleamed in triumph. Finally, his brother had come crawling to him begging for his life. Glancing at its contents, in the presence of all those who were there, he tore up the paper into tiny pieces and flung it aside.

Late that night, there were the sound of loud voices outside Dara's heavily guarded cell, and through the grill high in the cell door, Dara could see the lights from the flames of the torches grazing the vaulted roof of the passage that led to the cell. As the guards posted outside the cell unbolted its door, Dara threw a glance at Siphir, who with his head on his knees was in a fitful slumber, and then he rushed expectantly to the door, hoping against hope that they had been reprieved.

In a trice, half-a-dozen men, the lower part of their faces covered with a mask and armed with swords and knives, rushed in, and before Dara could react, they had pinioned his arms around his back.

Siphir rushed to protect his father, but he was torn from Dara's grasp and dragged away.

'Father, where are they taking me?' he cried as he was lifted off the ground and carried away struggling and screaming to another cell.

'What is...' That is all that Dara could cry out as a powerful pair of arms held him from behind, while a series of dagger thrusts ruptured his stomach. As he fell onto the floor, in a last bid to protect himself, he tried to reach out to a small dagger that he had kept concealed underneath the mattress, but that was wrenched away.

Meanwhile, the man who was leading the group swung his sword and Dara's head was severed from his body in a great rush of blood.

Late that night, Dara's head—placed on a salver and covered with a piece of cloth—was carried to Aurangzeb. 'Take it away,' he muttered when the attendants arrived with the ghoulish trophy. 'We hated seeing that infidel's face all the time he was alive, and do you think we want to see it, now that he is dead?'

Next morning, Dara's headless and horribly mutilated body, wrapped in cloth, was tied to the back of an elephant and then taken through the streets of Delhi to the lamentations of the population till it was interred unwashed, in some inconspicuous corner within the precincts of the tomb of his great-great-grandfather Humayun.

Epilogue

A few weeks later, one evening, as the sun was about to set, Alima Mooltani sat with some of her acolytes in the mango grove in the midst of a discourse.

'Enlighten us, Wise Teacher, to what extent is man the master of his own fortune, and how far does fate play a hand in man's life?' asked a young man as her discourse was about to conclude.

A smile played upon her lips and then she drew her two hands with their gnarled fingers, perhaps six inches apart. She held them there for a few seconds and then threw her arms wide open to close them a little while later.

'You get the point, my son?' she asked. 'Broadly speaking, no earthly being can escape the fate that lies in store for him. They are tablets written in stone and set out the path along which he is bound to tread. Yet, within that path which is predestined, the scope for free will is not entirely absent. Each of us is dealt with a set of cards, but how we play them is up to us. Take the case of Prince Dara, for instance, that unfortunate manner of whose death we have all heard about. Fate dealt him a hand which few mortals could hope to receive, and yet, due to indecision, arrogance and a failure to see the writing on the wall, he not only squandered it all, but also paid for it with his life. But then probably we judge him too harshly. It was perhaps the goodness of his heart that proved his undoing and made him lose his life to one who was in every way his inferior, except in deceit, craftiness and the use of the sword. Perhaps, a grander fate awaits Prince Dara, who will live forever in the hearts of men in his efforts to shed light on those underlying principles that form the bedrock of some of the world's great religions, than one could ever hope to achieve by arresting and deposing one's own father; sending into exile, arresting and murdering his brothers; and trampling on millions of human corpses to rule over an empire.'

Glossary

Advaita	A philosophy that believes in non-dualism
Alima	Lady possessing knowledge and learning
Dar al-Islam	Abode of Islam
Dargah	The shrine of a Muslim saint
Dastarkhwan	Dining spread
Divan	Used here to mean a couch
Diwan-e-Aam	Hall of public audience
Diwan-e-Khas	Hall of private audience
Fatiha	Opening sura of the Koran
Hakeem	Muslim doctor
Jagir	A type of feudal land grant
Jagirdar	Proprietor of an estate
Jharokha	Window
Jivatma	Soul that resides in living beings
Jizya	Poll tax that early Islamic rulers demanded from their non-Muslim subjects
Kasai tola	Butcher's colony
Khansama	Cook
Khanqah	A place where members of the Sufi faith meet and perform their spiritual rituals
Khillat	A robe of honour
Khuda Hafiz	May God protect you
Killedar	Commander of a fort

Kos	Distance measuring approx. 3.2 kilometres
Mansab	Rank or position
Mansabdar	A high-ranking Mughal official
Masalchi	Person who grinds condiments
Masnad	Couch
Mohtarma	Respected lady
Muezzin	Call to prayer
Mureed	Disciple
Naib Subedar	Deputy head of a province
Namaz	Muslim prayer
Pargana	District
Posta	Drug made from opium poppy
Qazi	Muslim judge
Quadriism	Belief in a Sufi order that developed in Baghdad in the twelfth century AD
Sajda	Bowing in prayer
Sarai	Rest house
Sarpech	A turban ornament
Shehnai	A musical instrument
Sowar	Cavalryman
Takht	The throne or the plank
Tauheed-e-Ilahi	Belief system that preaches oneness of God and life of virtue
Thikanedar	Proprietor of a smaller estate
Vishishtadvaita	A philosophy that qualifies non-dualism
Wali Ahad	Heir apparent

www.ingramcontent.com/pod-product-compliance
Lightning Source LLC
Chambersburg PA
CBHW020402030726
47496CB00007B/2263